THE TROUBLEMAKER

LILI VALENTE

THE TROUBLEMAKER

By Lili Valente

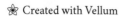 Created with Vellum

(HOT novellas, must be read in order)

Dark Domination

Deep Domination

Desperate Domination

Divine Domination

Kidnapped by the Billionaire Series

(HOT novellas, must be read in order)

Filthy Wicked Love

Crazy Beautiful Love

One More Shameless Night

Under His Command Series

(HOT novellas, must be read in order)

Controlling her Pleasure

Commanding her Trust

Claiming her Heart

To the Bone Series

(Sexy Romantic Suspense, must be read in order)

A Love so Dangerous

A Love so Deadly

A Love so Deep

Run with Me Series

(Emotional New Adult Romantic Suspense.

Must be read in order.)

Run with Me

Fight for You

The Bad Boy's Temptation Series

(Must be read in order)

The Bad Boy's Temptation

The Bad Boy's Seduction

The Bad Boy's Redemption

The Lonesome Point Series

(Sexy Cowboys written with Jessie Evans)

Leather and Lace

Saddles and Sin

Diamonds and Dust

12 Dates of Christmas

Glitter and Grit

Sunny with a Chance of True Love

Chaps and Chance

Ropes and Revenge

8 Second Angel

They say Rafe Hunter is trouble with a capital T.

I say—bring it on.

As long as Trouble comes in a package as delicious as Rafe's, I'm ready to climb on his Harley and ride all night long—and I'm not just talking about his motorcycle.

I can hide out until the scandal with my evil ex blows over AND have a wild rebound at the same time. Besides, I've got no heart left to break. My ex made sure of that.

As long as Rafe and I keep our no-strings fling from our families, what can possibly go wrong?

***

This is so damned wrong.

I don't do drama, and this thing with Carrie Haverford has Bad News written all over it. After one red-hot kiss, I know I should cut and run.

Instead I take her home, take her in her car, take her to the beach and make her scream louder than the crashing waves. And then I take her so far into my heart I don't see how I'm ever going to let her go.

The say the bigger and badder they are, the harder they fall. But when I fall for a girl with third degree love burns, how can I convince her that fire is a good thing?

This sexy Standalone romance will make you laugh, melt, and fall madly in love.

To Allison and G-haw,
fine practitioners of the Art of Trouble.

CHAPTER 1

RAFE

*W*eddings…

No offense to those who enjoy this kind of shit, but I'd rather be dragged naked through the streets behind a speeding Harley.

My brother's wedding is better than most—at the edge of a vineyard at sunset, with lights strung in the oak trees above the reception, and a live band playing bluegrass and golden-age love songs. And Dylan and Emma are crazy about each other and can't seem to stop having kids, so it makes sense for them to take the plunge, I guess, but the sappiness in the air is still making me queasy.

Romancing the shit out of a woman or fucking her until you're both too weak to stand is one thing. Getting teary-eyed over the wedding vows is another.

As soon as the toasts and the first dance are over, I beat it to the parking lot, knowing I won't be missed. The bride and groom are too busy making goo-goo eyes at each other, and everyone else is too drunk. The wedding started forty-five minutes late, and Emma's tasting room staff was pouring hefty samples while we waited.

I, however, only had one glass. I knew a quick getaway was in my future.

But when I reach my bike, I find my baby—a vintage 1950 Harley Panhead I coaxed back to glory with my own two hands—hemmed in by two Smart cars.

"What's Smart about an overpriced novelty baby stroller?" I grumble under my breath.

"Not to mention poor handling around corners, a less than stellar safety rating, and the fact that they look really, *really* stupid." The husky voice comes from the shadows beneath a live oak. A second later, the most dangerous blonde at the party steps into the light streaming from the lamps on the porch, looking as drop-dead sexy as ever.

With her shoulder-length blond hair dyed purple at the tips, thick eyeliner that accentuates her violet eyes, and a body made for the black leather bustier and long, gauzy skirt she's wearing, Carrie Haverford checks all of my boxes.

She's also Emma's sister and completely off-limits.

I don't have many rules when it comes to women, but I don't fuck where I eat, and I'll have to face my brother's sister-in-law over too many holiday dinner tables to risk a one-night stand.

Or however long we would last.

Judging by the sway of her hips as she slinks over to

sit on the hood of the red car in front of my bike, it wouldn't be long. She looks like a man-eater, this one.

Be still my raging hard-on...

I love bad girls who know what they want. They're even better than good girls desperate to prove how bad they can be with the right guy.

"Looks like you're stuck, bucko," Carrie says with a sigh. "I feel for you. I'm staying in Emma's guest cottage, so I'm also trapped in happily-ever-after-hell."

I laugh as I slide my hands into the pockets of my tux pants, the better to keep them to myself. "You hate weddings, too?"

"Like carpet burns on my ass," she says, filling my filthy mind with images of things I could do to her curvy body that would cause such a thing. "Marriage is just another sickness inflicted upon humanity by the development of agriculture. It's about property, not love everlasting." She flicks thick blond and purple locks off her forehead, revealing more of her doll-perfect face. "And people weren't intended to be monogamous. Science proved that years ago."

I arch a brow, intrigued. "Really? How's that?"

"Lots of different studies, but the most compelling to me is the design of your gear shift." Her gaze drops to the front of my pants before sliding slowly back up to meet my eyes.

"Yeah?" I murmur, getting thicker in spite of myself.

A hot body is reasonably easy to resist, but a sexy, shifty little mind like hers does me in every time.

"It's designed to suction out other men's deposits before making its own special delivery," she says, eyes dancing with mine, issuing a challenge I know I have to refuse. "We were meant to be wild things who don't give a damn if happy ever after is going to last a few hours, let alone a lifetime. The unity of the tribe was our focus, not locking one person in and weighing them down with all the expectations we used to expect a whole village to provide."

She shrugs. "And, allegedly, back when we were tribal nomads, we were less violent, too. The sperm did the fighting, and a woman's body chemistry controlled which got to make the baby, so there was no need for men to go to war over who controlled women and property. People could live in peace and spend their free time relaxing in waterfalls or digging grubs or whatever primitive people did for fun."

I grunt. "Sounds a lot more sane than the current arrangement."

Her eyes narrow as she nods. "Exactly. Why can't everyone else see that *they're* the crazy ones?" She crosses her arms with a sigh and a tragic shake of her head. "Why must they judge us, Valentine?"

I smile. "Everyone calls me Rafe. I told you that last time we met, Carrie."

"I don't care what everyone else does." She stands, hips swaying temptingly beneath her skirt as she moves closer. "I would rather call you Valentine Huxley Raphael, if that's all right."

I curse. "Who told you?"

"Dylan, when he was drunk at the brewery grand opening." She straightens the flower in my lapel, making me powerfully aware of how close she is and how incredible she smells. Like orange blossoms and spice. "Did you know your second name means 'inhospitable place,' Mr. Hunter?"

"But my first name means strong and healthy." I tip my head, bringing my mouth closer to hers. "And my third name means 'God has healed,' so I figure two out of three isn't bad. But there's a more pressing question on my mind right now, Trouble."

Her grin stretches wider, proving she likes it when people call her on her mischief. "Yes? What's that, Valentine?"

"Why have you been looking up the meaning of my many ridiculous names?"

"Why? Because I want to do bad things to you in the dark, silly," she says in a husky voice. She presses up onto tiptoe until our lips are barely an inch apart, and my pulse rushes faster. "What about you? Up for a top-secret night? You and me, nothing off-limits, and in the morning, we part ways and never say a word about it to each other or to anyone else ever again?"

I should say no.

I really, really should...

But I've never been good at "no" or "should," and she's making a compelling argument.

If we stick to Trouble's terms, what could go wrong?

So many things. Too many to name, starting with the extremely high probability of getting caught.

As if summoned by my thoughts, a feminine voice calls Carrie's name from the side of the house. Carrie's eyes go wide, and she takes a quick step back, putting a "just friends" amount of distance between us seconds before Emma appears by the front porch.

"Hey, there you are! And Rafe, too. Good!" She jogs across the drive, holding the hem of her wedding dress up out of the dirt. "Come on you two. We're getting ready to throw the bouquet and garter. We need all the single ladies and gentlemen in the garden."

Carrie makes a grumbling sound at the back of her throat. "You don't want me there, Em. It would be a waste of the bouquet if I caught it. You know I'm never getting married."

"Ditto," I say, also having exactly zero interest in holy matrimony. I can count the successfully married couples I know on two fingers, while the married and miserable, bitterly separating, or devastated and divorced crowd numbers in the dozens. The odds for marriage aren't good, and I'm not a gambling man. I take calculated risks, not wild leaps into nets full of holes.

Emma props a fist on her hip. "I know, I know, but we only have a few single people here. We need all the warm bodies we can get. Just stand in the back and make a half-hearted effort for the pictures, okay? For me? And then you can run off to get beer and play pool or whatever it was you guys were plotting out here."

"We have no plots," Carrie says, in a voice so innocent I almost believe her myself. "I was on my way back to the cottage to get some rest. It's been a long day."

"And I was trying to head home, but my bike is penned in." I nod over my shoulder, and Emma snorts.

"Well, that's fixed easily enough." She reaches out to

tug a lock of her sister's hair. "Just get the worst parallel parker in the universe to move her Mini Monster."

I glance at Carrie, arching a brow.

She lifts a bare shoulder and lets it fall, gaze shifting guiltily to the left.

"Or I can move it for you if you've had too much wine," Emma continues. "But I will only do so *after* you both play nice. So come with me my hopelessly un-romantics." She backs toward the house, beckoning for us to follow. "I promise—last wedding favor of the day, and then you're free."

"Be there in a second," Carrie says. "Just let me pop into the house and put on some lipstick."

"Two minutes," Emma warns.

"Two minutes," Carrie and I reply at the same time. Neither of us sounds overly excited, but apparently, lukewarm acquiescence is enough for Emma. She turns, starting down the path leading around to the garden, leaving Carrie and I alone.

After a beat, I ask, "So do you really hate your car, or was that just to throw me off the scent?"

"Both." She sighs. "And my plan would have worked, too, if it wasn't for those meddling kids."

I grin. "It was a solid plan."

"It was okay, for the spur of the moment." She gives her tire a half-hearted kick. "I can move it now if you want. Or you can. The keys are in the driver's seat."

"That's all right. Now that I think about it, I'll prob-ably walk up the hill and sleep at my dad's place." I slide my hands into my pockets as I turn to face her. "No sense in driving home just to turn around and drive back again first thing tomorrow for the wedding break-fast." I hesitate, forcing my eyes away from the enticing curves overflowing her top, willing myself to make the smart choice. "And no sense in sleeping anywhere else. Family can be friends, but anything more is a bad idea."

"It's called incest," Carrie says dryly. "But that's only if you're related by blood, not marriage."

"Still." I take a step backward, away from her spicy citrus scent and tempting mouth, which I bet would taste every bit as delicious as it looks. "See you at the bouquet toss?"

She nods. "Totally. See you there."

With a final smile, I turn and walk away, ignoring the pang of disappointment spreading through my balls.

Yes, I'm sure a night with Carrie would be hot as hell. But tomorrow morning we'd be smack dab in the "regrettable drama" part of the affair, sneaking around, trying not to get caught by our families, and wondering why we made things so unpleasant for ourselves. And even if we managed to avoid getting made, memories of the night would linger between us, festering and swelling like a balloon filled with botulism, primed to pop and spew poison all over our previously peaceful, uncomplicated family unit.

Better to walk away now.

Better to go to sleep alone and jerk off to ease this ache than to put my Carrie-Haverford-inspired hard-on to use with the woman herself.

Thanks to Emma, I dodged a bullet.

So, in the spirit of gratitude, I make an effort to catch the garter, reaching hard for the scrap of lace that ends up looped around my younger brother, Tristan's, fingers. But that's for the best. Tristan is going through a hard time in his love life, but he eventually wants to get married. Somehow, despite our identical upbringings, Tris ended up hopeful and open-hearted instead of jaded and convinced happily-ever-after is the biggest crock of shit society ever sold the collective unconscious.

But we both go home alone tonight, plodding up the hill in the dark to the farmhouse where we grew up, leaving the Haverford property behind.

And though I'm tempted, I don't look back at the lights shining in the tiny cabin at the edge of Emma's property or let my thoughts linger on the oh-so-tempting woman inside.

CHAPTER 2

CARRIE

*P*ublic speaking is the most common phobia in the world, and I get why. It's scary as hell to be up there alone, exposed to an audience full of people—but it's something I've gotten used to.

Since I was first published six years ago, requests for me to speak at schools have doubled and then tripled with the release of the fifth Kingdom of Charm and Bone book. Climbing onto a stage under glaring lights and discussing how I make the magic happen in my writer's brain shouldn't make me want to gnaw off my own arm with anxiety anymore. It shouldn't make my heart pound or my jaw ache or the valley of my spine become a trickling river of stress-sweat.

And maybe it wouldn't…if I were wearing clothes.

Or if my insides were still *inside* of me and my intestines weren't sliding out from a slit in my abdomen.

"So if you'll just um…direct your attention to slide

seven on the hero's journey," I say, pitch rising as I press my hands to the wound. But the slippery nightmare that is my lower digestive tract continues to escape through my fingers onto the worn wooden planks of Mendocino Middle School's theater stage.

Low muttering is already audible from the first few rows of people, who are no-doubt getting an eyeful of the zombie-apocalypse level of gruesome, and it's only a matter of time before the ruckus spreads. Soon the mutter will become chatter and the chatter a rumble and the rumble a roar of laughter as I trip over my own viscera and sprawl ass over elbows into the gaping maw of the open orchestra pit.

I've had this dream before.

I know how it's going to end.

I even have a pretty good idea what caused it— walking into the wrong labor and delivery room while my sister, Emma, was giving birth. Getting an eyeful of another woman's emergency C-section, which was just too gruesome for words, has scarred me for life and insured I take my birth control pill every morning with a fervor usually reserved for religious practice.

But knowledge won't stop the dream.

Just like my small, cold hands won't stop the flood pouring out quicker now, faster and faster until a little blond girl in the front row screams in horror and the principal shouts from the back of the auditorium —"What is the meaning of this, Ms. Haverford? This display isn't appropriate for children!"

"I know it's not appropriate," I shout back, terror

sweat pouring down my forehead to sting my eyes. "You think I planned this?"

"Disgraceful," a teacher with a prune mouth tuts from the front, where she's crouched down beside the girl, who is now sobbing into Pruney's ruffled shirt. "You ought to be ashamed of yourself."

"This is way too gross to be in a romance novel," another teacher pipes up from a few rows behind her, primly shoving her glasses up her nose.

"I don't write…romance," I pant, knees going weak as more of my insides become outsides and a deathly chill creeps into my bones. "I write fantasy adventure stories for kids."

"But there's romance in them," Prim argues, with a cock of her head.

"Beatrice and Levi are totally going to get together in the end." Pruney rolls her eyes as she strokes the little girl's heaving shoulders. "I knew that halfway through the first book. They'll have to if she wants to stay in the real world."

I start to tell Pruney that even *I* don't know how the series is going to end—I don't plot that far in advance—so there's no way *she* could know, but my lungs aren't cooperating. My lips are moving, but no sound is coming out, and the faces in the audience are starting to blur.

I take a step forward, reaching for the glass of water on the podium, naively hoping that it's not too late for hydration to make a difference. But as I move, I trip and tumble into the orchestra pit, diving head first into a strategically placed tuba—the way I do every time I have this dream—and the room explodes with laughter because a naked woman falling into a tuba is apparently hilarious, even if she's desperately in need of medical attention.

Or a viscera transplant.

Or a new brain, because clearly the old brain is tragically messed up.

* * *

"Oh my God." I bolt into a seated position in the sunny guest cottage, both hands clutching my abdomen through my sweat-soaked T-shirt. And like the crazy person I am, I lift up my shirt and stare at the unblemished skin near my hip for a good thirty seconds before I'm convinced it was all a dream.

"Just a dream." My breath rushes out in a mixture of frustration and relief. "Stop being a nutcase, Carrie. It was just a dream."

But, of course, it wasn't. Not entirely.

I might not have gone full horror-movie in front of hundreds of innocent children, but that probably would have played better in the press than what really happened. At the very least, I would be dead and liberated from my earthly worries, instead of hiding out in my sister's un-air-conditioned guest cottage in the dead of summer while the sun transforms the quaint, tiny home at the edge of her vineyard into a pressure cooker.

My brain already feels like a potato about to split its skin, and it's only nine o'clock in the morning.

Though I'm sure the multiple glasses of wine I drank last night in an attempt to enjoy my sister's breathlessly romantic wedding, while our mother glared at me every time I happened into her line of sight—Renee Haverford does not approve of racy bridesmaid's dresses or purple-tipped hair or any of the other decisions I've made since I was a toddler—might have something to do with the angry throb at my temples.

I definitely had a few too many.

My mouth feels like a desert wasteland, my eyes are puffy, and as I roll out of bed to stumble toward the mini fridge for a bottle of water, my stomach lets out a growl of protest, clamoring for something to assist in soaking up the Chardonnay still sloshing around inside it—ASAP.

I'm poking around in the shelves above the kitchen sink, nose wrinkling at all the healthy options Emma has so thoughtfully provided, when my cell bleats from the bedside table.

Thanks to the glory that is the tiny home, a crane of my neck allows me to see the text from my mother—

Renee: Breakfast starts in fifteen minutes. The rest of us are already having coffee and juice in the garden. Don't be late to your sister's wedding breakfast, Caroline.

With a hard eye-roll, I return to pawing through the fig paste, gluten-free, sprouted seed bars, and bundles of bulk nuts and dried fruit. The thought of trying to

14

ingest either coffee or juice makes my already irritable stomach bare its teeth in a warning snarl.

Nothing acidic.

I need bread, crackers, maybe some pretzels or—

Renee: And put on something decent that covers your shoulders. We haven't had a family picture in years. I'd like to get one with you girls before I'm too old to show up on film.

My mother labors under the delusion that she will *literally* become invisible after a certain age—like a vampire or a ghost. I've tried to explain to her that the "invisibility" of older women is a symptom of our diseased culture, which insists women are no longer worthy of being seen or heard once no one wants to fuck them anymore. But Renee isn't interested in my "man-hating" theories.

Though obviously, as evidenced by my many male friends and my sexual preferences, I don't hate men. I enjoy men—the feel of them, the taste of them, their simple, uncomplicated expectations and the way their brains work in linear pathways, without the confusing curves and coded messages ingrained in the communication of so many women I know.

If I could wake up tomorrow and be a man, I would do it in a heartbeat. Multiple orgasms are hardly adequate compensation for all the shit women have to put up with.

Bleeding every twenty-eight days, for example.

What asshole thought that was a good idea? And child-birth. Why must a child the size of a cantaloupe emerge from an exit the size of a celery stalk? Just so it hurts more? Because it increases the chances of a woman needing to be sliced open in order to fetch the squalling infant from its womb prison?

"Don't think about that," I groan as I settle on a package of dried dates and rip open the top of the bag, images from my dream dancing grotesquely through my head.

I pop a fig into my mouth and chew as I cross to the slim closet beside the bathroom and survey my selection of clean dresses. Nothing shoulder-covering, but I can borrow a shawl or something from Emma. Normally I would ignore my mother's requests, but I promised my big sister I would play nice with Mom while she's here staying in the big house and watching my niece while Emma and her husband, Dylan, head off for a short honeymoon.

I'm tugging out a sleeveless, brightly colored floral number that will pair well with just about any color shawl I can fetch from Emma's closet, when the landline rings loud enough to make me cry out and jump a foot into the air.

I lunge for it, snatching the receiver off the wall by the sink before it can ring again, and gasp, "I'm coming, Mom. Jesus, I'm on my way out the door right now."

"It's not Mom, it's me." My sister's sweet voice is hushed and urgent. "Just wanted to warn you not to turn on the TV. Don't check your email, either. There's nothing you can do about it right now, and I want you to enjoy your breakfast. I bought the chocolate and raspberry croissants you love, and you deserve to eat them in peace."

I sit down on the edge of the bed, dress clutched too tightly in my hand. "What happened? Just tell me. Get it over with."

"No," Emma insists. "I don't want to talk about it. This entire situation makes me so angry I want to stab someone, and I already want to stab Mom. If I get any more keyed up, I might do violence to her with my butter knife and have to spend my honeymoon in prison."

"What did she do this time?"

"She said I needed to put Mercy on a diet." Emma bites the words out. "She thinks my thirteen-month-old daughter needs to watch her figure."

I roll my eyes so hard the room starts to spin. "Ignore her. She's insane. Mercy is perfect, and perfectly healthy, and I'll make sure Renee doesn't starve her while you're gone. Just remember it all stems from Mom's own insecurities and that she's in more pain than she'll ever cause the rest of us."

"You're generous with her," Emma grumbles.

"Not really. I've just learned to choose my battles. Hang in there, and I'll be over to offer moral support in ten minutes. As soon as I get dressed and find out what you're refusing to talk to me about."

Emma sighs. "Fine. Apparently, the story broke on TMZ last night. It's everywhere, Carrie, on all the entertainment blogs and getting picked up by some mainstream news sources. I'm sorry."

I drop my head into my free hand, eyes squeezed shut. "It's okay. I sort of figured this would happen. It would have been more surprising if a story that juicy had stayed buried. It's not every day a children's book author shows her nude photos to an auditorium full of middle school kids."

"But it wasn't your fault!" Emma protests. "You didn't put those pictures in your presentation. Jordan's the one to blame. He's the bad guy. You're innocent."

"Hardly. I posed for the pictures. In some people's minds that's enough to make me guilty. Children's books authors should keep their clothes on at all times, Emma. Even when bathing."

Emma snorts. "That's ridiculous. Just because you write for children doesn't mean you're not a grown-up with a sex life. People contain multitudes. And I've always thought it was great that you're confident in your body. I wish I had the ovaries to pose for sexy pictures. You look beautiful in them, by the way, if that's any consolation."

I freeze, my blood going cold. "You've seen them? How? How did you see them?"

"Oh shit," Emma says with a rush of breath.

I lift my head, eyes going wide as my foggy brain puts the pieces together.

"Forget I said that," Emma hurries on. "Forget I even called and come have breakfast."

"He leaked the pictures to the press?" I stand, pacing back and forth in the narrow corridor between the bed and the kitchenette. "I can't believe he did that! What? Tanking the public-speaking side of my career wasn't enough? He had to show the entire world my weird nipples?"

"They are not weird."

"They're skinny and crooked, Emma. They're weird," I screech, as my throat gets tighter, tighter, until it feels like anxiety is a boa constrictor looped around my neck.

"They're jaunty and perfectly shaped and you're beautiful. But more importantly, we shouldn't be having this conversation because Jordan should have kept private things private instead of being an evil bastard who violated the trust that was placed in him."

I shove another date into my mouth and whimper around it, "Shit, Emma. What am I going to do? How am I ever going to show my face in public again? I'm going to have to hide out here for the rest of my life."

"You are not," Emma says, steel creeping into her tone. "You have nothing to be ashamed of. You will take the time you need to heal and then you'll come out swinging, as usual. Now get over here and get a croissant before they're all gone."

I whimper again but manage to gather the strength to shove my PJ pants to the floor and step into my dress.

"We'll eat, enjoy the sunshine, and tackle next steps later," she continues. "My plane doesn't leave until late this afternoon. We'll have plenty of time to make a game plan after the boys leave."

"The boys..." I echo, a prickling sensation rippling through my brain.

"Dylan's brothers, nephews, and Dad are all here," Emma says. "Father Pete, too."

Oh no, Dylan's brothers...

Including the brother I propositioned last night.

Shit!

"I can't come to breakfast." I sink to the floor, knocking a fist into my stupid forehead.

"Yes, you can."

I squinch my eyes closed. No, I can't. I can't face Rafe, not now. Rejection is a bitter pill to swallow on a good day, one where your nude pictures haven't just been wallpapered all over the Internet. And cable TV. And wherever else the news has spread.

God, what was I thinking? Yes, Rafe is exactly the no-strings kind of guy a girl needs to help bang an ugly breakup out of her system, but he's also my *brother-in-law*. He's off-limits. I've known that since the moment I met him, and not even four glasses of Chardonnay should have made me forget it.

I groan again as I remember saying something about his "gear shift" and holding forth on how humans are biologically designed to have multiple partners.

And yeah, it's all true, but it's not the kind of conversation you make with family. Because you don't have casual sex with family, not even family by marriage. As tight as Emma's husband is with his brothers and I am with Emma, Dylan's family might as well be mine. I'm going to be seeing a lot of these people for a lot of years to come, and now I've ensured that I'll be mortified in front of at least one of them for the foreseeable future.

Oh hell, who am I kidding? As soon as the Hunter men see the pictures, I'll never be able to look any of them in the eye, ever again.

"Are you listening? I swear, if you're not here in five

minutes, I'm coming to chase you out of the house with the garden hose," Emma says, her voice loud enough to be heard over the chaos filling my head. "We're all family here, and there's no reason to be embarrassed in front of family."

Before I can reply, a voice in the background calls out, "You coming, Em? I'm serving the eggs and bacon. Mercy's so hungry she's eating the flowers again."

"Be there in just a second, honey," Emma calls back before admonishing me, "And you be here in a second, too. No more of this nonsense. Come get fed, and then we'll form a diabolical plan for revenge. Jordan's not going to get away with this, not if I have anything to say about it."

Emma hangs up and I drop the phone onto the bed.

For a second, I debate getting in my car and making a run for it, but I have nowhere to run to.

I can't go home to my apartment in Berkeley. There were already reporters sniffing around before I left. After this morning's bombshell, I'm sure it's going to be even worse. I can't go to any of my writer friends' houses because they work from home and are too busy to deal with my nonsense—or are hermit creatures who refuse to get out of their pajamas, leave the house, or engage with other people more than once or twice a week, and would therefore see my visit as a violation of their basic human rights. And I can't go to my mom or dad's because mom and I are not on house-sharing terms and my father is a disgusting pig-person who is basically living with his goat herd and everything in his place reeks of billy goat pee.

That's why I'm here at Emma's. Not only because she's the person I'm closest to, but because she's the *only* person willing to offer me shelter in my time of need.

I'm thirty years old and the list of people I can truly count on is one-person long. I receive dozens of emails from fans every week, I've sold hundreds of thousands of copies of my books and hit the New York Times bestseller list twice, but from a real life, boots on the ground perspective, I'm one step away from being a weirdo loner who wanders the streets talking to the imaginary people living in my head.

It makes me wonder if I've been doing this whole "life" thing all wrong...

At that moment, my phone bleats again.

Renee: You're ruining your sister's wedding breakfast. I knew this would happen.

Shockingly, the text makes the backs of my eyes sting and my chest ache. And here I thought I was long past the point where anything Renee said could make me cry.

Guess not...

But damn if I'm going to let her know her dart found a hole in my armor.

Instead, I change out of my relatively modest flower dress into a pair of tiny black short-shorts and a skimpy lavender tank top that matches the highlights Renee hates in my hair, smear on thick black eyeliner, pull on my combat boots and my T.Rex ring, and head into battle with my jaw set and my emotions under lock and key.

This may be the first time I've had nude photos leaked to the public, but I learned a long time ago how to pretend my heart wasn't breaking.

At that, like public speaking, I have become a fucking pro.

CHAPTER 3

RAFE

*S*o far, so good…

The eggs and bacon have been dispersed, and we're passing around the pastry plate, but there's still no sign of Carrie. If my luck holds, I'll be able to wolf down breakfast, plead urgent work at the shop as an excuse to leave early, wish Dylan and Emma a happy start to many years of wedded bliss, and get out of here before another encounter with Emma's sister.

We escaped disaster last night, but if I have to spend much more time in Carrie Haverford's violet-eyed, plush-lipped, sexy-as-hell presence, I'm going to do something I'll regret. Like invite her onto the back of my bike, drive out to my favorite secluded, oceanside cliff, and fuck her senseless on the blanket I keep in my saddlebag.

I spent half the night dreaming about her curves stretched out on soft gray wool, her legs spread to welcome my mouth between her thighs, her gorgeous body rippling beneath mine as my gear shift and I gave her the ride of her life.

I would *very* much like to make Carrie Haverford come screaming my name—pleasuring a woman who has the experience to appreciate an extraordinary lay is something I find very fucking satisfying. But if I stick my dick in my sister-in-law's sister, I'll be giving drama a handwritten, engraved invitation, and that's just not my style.

"How are your eggs?" Dylan asks, nudging my elbow with his.

"Good," I say around a mouthful of bacon. "Gone."

"I noticed. I haven't seen you eat this fast since you quit wrestling junior year." My brother sighs. "Guess you're aiming to get out of here before the shit hits the fan?"

I glance his way, brows lifting. Concern tickles the hairs at the back of my neck, but I ignore it. There's no way Dylan knows what almost happened with Carrie last night. Whatever he's talking about, it has nothing to do with me.

"You haven't heard?" He shakes his head before continuing in a softer voice, "Carrie's ex leaked nude pictures of her to the press."

My eyes go wide and anger flares hot and sudden in my chest. "What the fuck? What kind of piece of shit does that?"

"The kind who doctored her PowerPoint presentation so nude photos popped up on the screen while she was giving a talk to some middle school kids last week,"

Dylan says, frowning as I start to choke on my orange juice. "You didn't know?"

I shake my head with a cough. "No."

"That's why Carrie moved into our guest cottage. She was hoping if she stayed off the grid, the scandal would blow over. But now her ex has taken it to the next level."

I curse softly, the urge rising inside me to find this coward and punch his balls so far into his abdomen he'll still be digging them out next Christmas. But I stopped tackling problems with my fists years ago and Carrie's problems aren't mine to solve.

Still, I can't help wondering... "So what's next? Is she going to take legal action?"

Dylan shrugs as he stabs another bite of scrambled eggs. "I'm not sure. It just happened a couple of hours ago. Emma's going to talk to her after breakfast. I don't know what they'll decide, but if it were up to me, we'd absolutely lawyer up and go after this guy. Embarrassing her is bad enough, but he's deliberately trying to wreck her career while he's at it."

I'm about to agree with him when Emma appears behind Dylan's chair, a sticky-faced, syrup-drenched blond cherub in her arms. "Mercy got ahold of the syrup again," she says breathlessly, as my niece giggles and thrashes her arms and legs, clearly pleased with herself and the mess she's made. "Can you help me get her out of these clothes and into the bath?"

"On it." Dylan tosses his napkin on the table as he stands. "You start the water, I'll get her out of her dress and put it in the sink to soak."

The happy couple hurries into the house while the wedding party continues to feast upon eggs, bacon, pastries, and several pounds of fresh fruit and berries. My dad is holding court at the far end of the table, torturing my nephews and their girlfriends with stories from his glory days, while my oldest brother, Deacon, shovels it in with the single-minded focus of a lifelong military man accustomed to eating far inferior food. Next to Deacon, Emma's mother flirts with Farmer Stroker, even though our eighty-year-old neighbor is ancient enough to be her father. Closer to my end of the table, beside Emma's empty chair, my younger brother Tristan speaks earnestly with the minister who married Emma and Dylan, both of them looking far too somber for people celebrating the union of a couple who are madly in love.

But the minister—Father Pete, a family friend who went to school with Deacon before going to Episcopal seminary—is getting a divorce, and my brother recently broke up with his girlfriend of over a decade. I doubt either of them feel much like celebrating, and though I respect Pete and love my baby brother, I don't want to get sucked into whatever sad-clown fest they're having.

I would prefer not to get sucked into *any* further conversation, as a matter of fact, and with Dylan and Emma gone and everyone else engaged, I sense the moment to escape is at hand.

After wiping my mouth discreetly, I place my napkin beside my empty plate, take a last drink of fresh OJ, and slide from my chair. I slip around the tall shrubs at the edge of Emma's impressive garden, and a moment later I'm out of sight, following the paving stone trail around to the front of the house, making a mental note to text Dylan and thank him for breakfast when I get home.

He won't mind that I bailed without a formal good-bye. Dylan and I might only be half-brothers, but we've been best friends since we were five years old. He knows ghosting is part of who I am, and not a part I'm ever going to apologize for. Goodbyes aren't my thing, especially big family goodbyes that take half an hour to get everyone out the door.

My bike is parked by the house for an easy getaway, and I'm nearly home free when a flash of light and color on the porch draws my focus.

I glance over, meeting a lavender-blue gaze so sad the emotion reverberates through my chest like a mallet lobbed into a drum. Immediately, I slow, turning to face the woman huddled in the red rocking chair with her knees drawn in to her chest.

Yes, I was hoping to make my escape without seeing Carrie, but I can't leave her like this—braced for the next bomb to hit and clearly on the verge of tears.

"Hey." I prop my hands low on my hips. "Not up for breakfast?"

She shakes her head. "I was headed that way, but then my agent's assistant texted to tell me my speaking gigs for the rest of the summer have been cancelled, so..."

I sigh. "I heard about what happened. What your ex did. I'm sorry."

Carrie winces as her focus drops to the dusty

ground at my feet. "Thanks. So… I guess everyone has seen them, then? The pictures?"

"I haven't. And I won't go looking," I assure her. "No one here will."

"Thanks." Her lips twist. "But I'm sure my mom is going to hunt them down. And when she sees them, I'm going to get a lecture about the importance of professional lighting, especially when taking one's clothes off, and why I should stop trusting people because I'm a shit judge of character."

Hmmm… Mom issues. Not surprising from what I've seen of her mother so far, but definitely not something I want to get into. I don't do issues. I offloaded mine in junior high, perfected not giving a shit in high school, and embraced the Zen lifestyle fully as an adult. Not sweating life's bullshit is something I take pride in, and a trait I seek out in other people.

If you're looking for a shoulder to cry on, I'm not your man, not by a long shot.

I'm about to say something kind but vague—*sorry again, hope things get better*, or some such—when Carrie stands, stretching her arms high over her head, causing her breasts to strain the front of her pale purple tank top.

My mouth goes dry and my pulse picks up, throbbing in my throat. God, she's beautiful. Perfectly made from the tip of her button nose to the tips of all the other parts that I shouldn't be *thinking* about, let alone openly drooling over.

Exerting more willpower than I would like, I wrench my gaze from her chest as her arms fall to her sides.

"Forget it," she says. "I don't want to talk about this shit, and I'm sure you don't, either. And I can handle breakfast. I have to handle it." She sighs as she jabs a thumb toward the driveway. "When I moved my car last night, I guess I didn't shut the door all the way after. Stupid battery is dead. Until I get a jump, I'm trapped."

Trapped. It's one of my least favorite things in the world. And judging from her tone, I'm guessing it's not high on her list, either.

"But you'd rather run?' I ask. "If you had the chance?"

She huffs a soft, "Oh yeah. Much rather."

I let out a measured breath, weighing my options. The smart thing would be to tell her goodbye and good luck, jump on my Harley, and get the hell out of here before I do something I'll regret. The kinder choice would be to give her a jump and send her on her way alone, ensuring she has the juice to run as far and as fast as she needs to in order to escape the misery weighing her down.

But when her full lips tremble and her violet eyes begin to shine, I find myself jerking my head toward my bike. "Come on. Let's go for a ride."

She blinks, shoulders rolling away from her ears as she stands up straighter. "Really?"

"Really. I've got an extra helmet and nowhere special to be."

With a soft yip of excitement, she jumps over the porch railing to land lightly on the ground in front of me. A moment later, her arms are around my neck, her curves pressing against my chest as she locks me into a surprisingly powerful hug. "Thank you, Rafe. Really. I appreciate it. I could use a friend this morning."

"No problem." I return the embrace with one arm, trying not to notice how perfectly she fits against me or how amazing she smells. She said it herself—she needs a friend, which is perfect because that's all she and I are ever going to be.

Carrie and I are friends.

Friends, I repeat silently as she settles onto the bike behind me, her thighs sliding against mine, her arms locking around my waist, and her breasts soft and tempting against my back.

Friends don't give friends raging erections, asshole.

The inner voice is right, of course. But my dick doesn't give two shits about right or wrong, and by the time we pull out onto the highway, I'm as hard as a steel pike and not sure who will win out in a battle of wills—the logical inner voice or the hunger curling low and tight inside me, whispering that sometimes rules are meant to be broken.

CHAPTER 4

CARRIE

e roar down deserted back roads, past vineyards shrouded in morning mist, hushed redwood forests, and ancient orchards heavy with midsummer fruit. Soon the only things on my mind are an awareness of how incredible the fresh air feels buffeting my skin, and a terrified voice at the core of my brain assuring me that I'm *ABOUT TO FUCKING DIE!*

Despite my long-standing rebellious tendencies, I've never actually ridden on a motorcycle before. Most of my friends are artists and musicians who need cars large enough to carry their art and music-making supplies, or book nerds like me who are cautious by nature and can't help memorizing odd bits of information—like the terrifying statistics on motorcycle-related crashes each year.

The closest I've ever been to tearing up the road

Harley style was on a rented moped that tapped out at twenty-five miles per hour.

But as Rafe guides his sleek machine out of the cool Green Valley hollows into the full sun on the highway toward Santa Rosa, we're going at least fifty.

Maybe sixty.

Seventy-five, the hysterical voice screeches. *When you hit the pavement, you'll splatter on impact. They'll have to put you back together like a jigsaw puzzle for the funeral. They may never find your eyeballs!*

I press my face against Rafe's back, inhaling the soap and leather smell of him, focusing on the assured way he directs the bike purring between our thighs. He's clearly a man who's at ease—and at one with—his machine. He's in command, in control, and I'm not in any danger.

At least not in danger of imminent splatterment.

There are other dangers, of course…

The risk inherent in leaving my hiding place and venturing out into the world, where people are, in record numbers this very morning, learning what I look like naked. The risk of spending quality time with a man who isn't on board with a low-key hookup, despite the way his gaze lasered in on my chest while I was on the porch.

Damn, but I liked being looked at like that. By him. The heat in his eyes was enough to make my nipples hard and my nerve endings sizzle, but Rafe made it clear that he wants to stay in the friend zone.

And I'm *fine* with that…in theory.

But considering that every time we touch electricity

leaps between us, his eyes go dark and sexy, and my mind floods with X-rated thoughts, I don't know how long we'll be able to be good. And if we're bad, Rafe might come to regret me, maybe even resent me, and I really don't want that to happen.

I was telling the truth—I really could use a friend, especially one who isn't so close to my issues. My sister is an incredible ally, but she's also the most empathetic person on earth. Emma feels your pain all the way down to her marrow. Looking into her eyes and seeing your inner torment reflected back in high definition can just be too much.

Sometimes it's nice to be with someone who's content to ignore the elephant in the room and just watch some mindless television or—

"You subscribe to the paper?" I hop off the bike in back of Rafe and Dylan's motorcycle repair shop-slash-microbrewery. Both are closed for the long weekend while Emma and Dylan are on their honeymoon, but Rafe lives in the two-bedroom apartment above.

He bends to scoop the paper off the stoop before fitting his key in the door. "I do. I like to know what's happening in the world without some twenty-four-hour news station turning everything into a crisis."

"Me, too," I say, following him up a long, narrow staircase. "And I like the feel of it between my fingers. It's so much more relaxing than reading online, and there are no eerily-relevant ads flashing in the sidebar reminding me that the bots are spying on me."

"I hate that," Rafe agrees. "Another reason I stay offline as much as possible."

We reach the top of the stairs, and the space opens up into a large, airy apartment with lofted ceilings, exposed beams, and loads of light streaming in through windows overlooking the street below. There's an enormous, overstuffed brown couch that looks cozy as hell, a leather coffee table perfect for spreading out the paper on, and a fan spinning lazily overhead that will keep the air cool as the morning warms up. It's the perfect oasis of calm, and if I weren't worried about starting things we shouldn't finish, I would feel compelled to give Rafe another hug.

Instead, I smile and say, "Love your place."

"Thanks. Simple, clean, and comfortable. That's all I've got in the way of style."

"I like it." I'm about to suggest reading time and ask if I might presume upon his hospitality by making us a pot of coffee, when he grunts and dumps the Chronicle into the recycling container at the top of the stairs.

"We should skip the paper today." He moves into the room, toward the kitchen on the far side of the space. "I've got yesterday's lying around somewhere. I didn't have a chance to read it before the wedding."

"What? Why?" I ask, but then I catch a glimpse at the front page, peeking out of the recycling bin, and I know exactly why he's chosen to pitch the paper.

"Oh no..." I crouch to read the headline aloud. "Bay Area author suspected of sexual misconduct? But I didn't do anything sexual! I didn't do anything at all!" I drive my fingers into my helmet-flattened hair as I sit down hard on his polished hardwood floors. "How is this spiraling out of control so fast?"

Rafe retraces his steps, sitting down next to me and pushing the recycling bin out of reach. "Do you need to call someone? A lawyer, maybe?"

"I-I don't think so." I bring my thumb to my mouth, nibbling at the rough spot near the edge. "Sensational headlines can say whatever they want, but I truly *didn't* do anything wrong. Certainly, nothing that could result in criminal charges." I hum, tapping the toes of my boots together as I think. "But I should probably get my agent to put a better spin on this, maybe help me hire a publicist. But he's on a yoga retreat in Mexico with no Internet and won't be back until Wednesday, and I don't trust his assistant to know who would be best for a job like this."

"You could reach out to Emma," Rafe suggests gently. "She gives good advice."

I shake my head. "No. I told you, I don't want to talk. Talking is dumb."

"Talking *is* dumb, but sometimes it's necessary to keep from exploding."

"I'm not going to explode."

"You sure about that?" he asks, eyeing me warily.

I wrap my arms tight around my shins and hunch my shoulders. "Yes, I'm sure. Emma is enjoying her wedding breakfast. I feel bad enough for skipping it. The last thing I want to do is dump more rain on her parade." Resting my chin on my knees, I add in a softer voice, "And most of my friends are friends with Jordan, too, and I don't think I could handle it if they've decided to take his side."

"He doesn't have a side," Rafe says. "He's an asshole."

I shrug as I glance up at him. "I'm sure *he* thinks he has a side. Even bad guys are good guys in their own heads, you know? They usually have what they believe are justifiable reasons for being awful."

The furrow between Rafe's brows deepens. "There is no justification for leaking private pictures. It doesn't matter if the relationship is over, or how badly it ended, the trust that was given should still be sacred."

"Yeah, well…" I swallow past the lump forming in my throat. "Maybe you wouldn't feel that way if you knew the whole story."

"Doubtful. But run it by me." Rafe shifts into a cross-legged position facing me. "I'm not much of a talker, either, but I'm a good listener."

I shake my head self-consciously. "No, it's okay. Really. I appreciate the offer, but it would be weird. *I* would be weird. I'm an advice-giving champ, but I don't do the unburdening thing myself very often. I worry too much about unguarded words coming back to haunt me."

He nods, eyes narrowing as he hums. "I know what you need."

Mindless, hot-and-heavy sex so intense it will scald this nightmare from my thoughts for a few hours?

Aloud I ask, "What?" in a wary tone.

"You need the teepee of silence."

I arch a skeptical brow.

"You do," Rafe insists. "The teepee of silence was where my brothers and I used to go when we needed to let loose about something private. What's shared in the teepee stays in the teepee. You can say anything, and no one will judge you or tell you to shut up or rat you out to the people in charge."

"Too bad we don't have a teepee handy," I joke, though the concept does sound kind of nice. Sort of like therapy, but with people who love you instead of a person you're paying to sit there and ask you how your shitty childhood makes you feel.

Why, it makes me feel shitty, doctor! Imagine that.

"That's okay. We can improvise." Rafe stands and reaches a hand down to me. "Help me grab blankets and pillows. My couch isn't as big as the one my dad had when we were kids, but it's big enough for a blanket fort built for two."

My lips curve in spite of myself. "I haven't built one of those in years. Not since Emma and I made a fort to watch scary movies in one Halloween when I was..." I trail off with a shake of my head. "God, I don't even know. Maybe eight or nine? Still young enough to be terrified by *Cujo*. And *Firestarter*. And the bad guys in the Care Bears movie."

Rafe grins. "No scary movies or Care Bears in this fort, I promise."

I sigh, my smile fading. Horror movies would be far less scary than what Rafe's proposing we get up to in this therapy teepee, but I can't deny a part of me does want to talk, to let off some of the pressure. And though I don't know Rafe that well, I trust him to keep his word about something like this.

"Come on, you'll feel better after." Rafe curls his fingers, beckoning me forward into the unknown.

"I'm not sure about that, but I guess I don't have

much left to lose." I take his big, warm hand, letting him pull me to my feet.

And yes, awareness surges between us again, thickening the air with dangerous possibilities, making my lips tingle and my skin heat. But there is something new simmering beneath the surface now, too, something that feels like the first, tentative flickers of real friendship. Rafe is every bit the devil-may-care bad boy, but he's got a heart under all the worn leather and faded denim.

Maybe even a good heart.

As I follow him to his hall closet and help pull out every blanket, fleece, and quilt in his personal collection, I try to avoid noticing how his jeans cling to his powerful thighs or the sexy stubble darkening his jaw. I keep my thoughts aboveboard and above the waist, the way a friend should. Because if Rafe is the guy I'm starting to think he is, I want him in my corner for the long haul. Good-hearted friends are worth their weight in gold and not worth risking on something as fleeting as a few world-rocking orgasms.

Though I'm sure they would have been world-rocking. Even the way the man arranges pillows is sensual and assured, carnal and powerful, and when he cocks his head and asks, "Ready to head inside?" in a husky voice, I can't help wishing we were crawling into bed instead of into a blanket fort in the middle of his living room.

But I am a grown woman in control of myself, so I simply nod and say, "As ready as I'll ever be," and drop to my knees.

CHAPTER 5

RAFE

*I*nside the blanket fort, the light is soft and warm, diffused by vintage flower-power sheets from the 1970s I grabbed from my mom's attic the last time I was in Sacramento.

As Carrie settles cross-legged onto a pillow beside me beneath our linen ceiling, her skin glows in the golden light. She looks like she just stepped out of a sixteenth-century Italian painting—a naughty shepherdess taking a break from watching her sheep—and I'm possessed by the urge to lean over and press a kiss to her bare shoulder. To slide the strap of her tank top down her arm. To roll her beneath me and explore every inch of her soft skin with my mouth.

Instead, I curl my fingers into fists that I rest on my knees, determined *not* to make physical contact.

We're walking the friend path. It might be hard now, but every step we take toward being buddies is a step away from temptation. Soon I'll be able to look at

Carrie and see just another woman friend—like Emma, or Sophie from the coffee shop—and this gut-twisting hunger will be a distant memory.

Right. And when you wake up tomorrow morning, you'll have grown a third eye and be able to see into the future.

Ignoring the weak-willed voice of doom, I nod Carrie's way. "We are in the blanket fort of silence. Let anything and everything shared within these walls stay within these walls."

Carrie shifts on her pillow, nibbling at her bottom lip in a way that does nothing to banish my urge to bite her pretty mouth. "And what happens when the walls fall down?"

"The secrets go back into the cupboard with them. Scout's honor."

"Were you a Boy Scout?" she asks, lips quirking. "Really?"

"No, I was a Future Farmer of America, which is even more trustworthy," I say. "Because farmers feed people, while Boy Scouts worry about collecting badges. Now quit trying to change the subject and get the shit off your chest."

Her breath rushes out, her small but perfectly-shaped breasts rising and falling beneath her thin shirt, and I immediately regret mentioning her chest. *Do not talk about her chest, do not look at it, do not think about it,* I remind myself, forcing my gaze to her face as she begins to speak.

"Jordan and I met at a children's book conference. He illustrated one of my favorite books that year, he was a fan of my work, and we got to talking over drinks. I ended up offering to mentor him on his first novel. He wanted to move on from illustrating, expand his career opportunities, and I thought I could help."

"That was generous," I say. "I've done some mentoring for the kids at the local high school who are interested in engine repair. It's not always easy."

She shakes her head. "No, it's not, but Jordan was an adult with a lot of experience in the industry, not a kid or a newbie. So I thought it would be fairly easy. And it was, until we started sleeping together and things got… more confusing."

"Confusing how?" I prod after a moment.

"He started feeling entitled to my time in a way he hadn't before," she says, picking at a loose thread on the quilt. "He wanted more critique but wouldn't put anything I said to use. It started to feel like he just wanted me to rewrite the chapters for him. So…I did, until it got to the point where I was contributing so much that I didn't feel comfortable moving forward without my name attached to the project."

"That makes sense," I say, hating this guy even more than I did before. I can see where this story is going, and I don't like it. Not a fucking bit. "But he didn't think you deserved credit, I'm guessing? He thought he should be able to take your work and pass it off as his own?"

Her shoulders inch toward her ears. "Pretty much. He said the story idea was his and that's what mattered, but that's not true. Character and plot matter, the voice of the piece matters, and that voice was mine. He wanted to take those things for free. He felt I owed it to him to prove I cared about our relationship."

"I'm hoping you called bullshit."

"Um, yeah," she says. "I called bullshit and informed him that having my name on his first effort as a writer would be a benefit since I had a large, established readership." She rolls her eyes. "He said I was an egomaniac who let my hubris consume everyone and everything around me and that if I wasn't careful I would find myself alone, friendless, and loveless for the rest of my life."

My scowl deepens. "Charmer. Glad you kicked his ass to the curb."

"But that's the thing...I didn't." Her shoulders slump as her fingers tangle in her lap. "That's part of the reason I'm so pissed at myself. I kept seeing him, trying to work it out personally and professionally and come to a compromise we could both live with." She shakes her head. "And then he submitted the manuscript to a publishing house behind my back, without my name on it. I found out when we were out to drinks with friends and he announced that he'd gotten a five-figure deal for his first novel."

"Motherfucker."

"No, he wouldn't do that," she says with a crooked grin. "He's repulsed by women who have children, which makes the fact that he illustrates books for kids even more grossly ironic."

I cross my arms, remembering why I hate drama. Even hearing about it secondhand makes my heart punch at my ribs and my fists itch to smash things. "I hope this isn't the end of the story. Douchebag gets a publishing deal and then drops some revenge porn

43

while you hide out at your sister's place? Because that story sucks."

Her cheeks flush. "No, it's not. I'd saved every draft of the book that I'd worked on, with my changes tracked. I got in touch with my agent, who got in touch with the publisher, and pretty soon Jordan didn't have a book deal anymore. Or a steady date. I cleaned out his drawer and dumped it on his front porch with a note encouraging him to stop being a piece of shit."

I nod, the tension easing from my arms. "Good."

"No, not good. The note was mean. Very mean." She winces, baring clenched teeth. "He showed it to some of our friends, who didn't know the whole story, and all of a sudden they wouldn't return my calls. And before I had a chance to explain myself, Jordan hacked into my cloud drive and replaced my school presentation PowerPoint with one featuring naked pictures of me. But of course, I had no idea that's what he'd done until I was standing in front of a hundred middle school kids while a picture of me naked in a claw-foot bathtub flashed on the screen behind me and every teacher in the place started gasping like a fish out of water."

"Damn." My jaw clenches as a cringe takes possession of my entire body, head to toe.

"Yeah, right? That's pretty much what I did."

"And then you ran? Grabbed your shit and got out of there?"

A laugh escapes her lips. "Um, no. I stayed, actually. I mean, I ripped the plug out of the wall and slammed my laptop closed and got the naked woman off the screen as fast as I could, but..." Her shoulders bob. "Fifty of those kids had already bought books. And more had brought books from home they wanted me to sign. I couldn't run away and leave them hanging and disappointed."

I lean back, bracing my arms on the floor behind me. "Wow. You've got balls, woman. Balls of steel."

She grins, a shy grin I've never seen before, one that makes a dimple pop in her cheek which is fucking adorable. "No, I don't. I'm just good at faking it. And I hate letting people down. Especially little people. I don't want to be one of those grown-ups who teaches kids that promises can't be trusted."

I nod, respect for her blooming. "I get it. And I'm with you."

Carrie looks up, studying me through her lashes. "Really? It doesn't seem like it."

"Why's that?" I ask, fighting to keep from getting sucked into her eyes. They're a color that immediately draws attention—more violet than blue—but it's the fire and intelligence in her gaze that gets to me. That makes me want to get closer, closer, until I've veered out of the friend zone and am headed way out-of-bounds.

"You think I should have stayed for the rest of it, too," she says softly. "That I should have held my ground and fought for my life and my friends instead of running off to hide in my sister's cottage."

I stretch my legs out with a shake of my head. "Nope. I'm not here to judge. That's not part of the blanket fort of silence. I'm just here to listen."

She cocks her head. "Really? You can listen without judging?"

"Most of the time. I don't like anyone telling me how I should live. That makes it easy to return the favor."

Carrie blinks as respect rearranges her features. "That's wonderful. And appreciated. Thanks for that. And thanks for making the fort. I do feel better." She sighs, her nose scrunching. "Even though I still have no idea what to do next. Or why Jordan's made it his mission in life to destroy my reputation."

"Because he thinks you took something that was his," I say, the motivation behind this weasel's hate seeming pretty clear to me. "So he's trying to take something that's yours."

"My entire career. My friends. My place in the community." She blows out a breath, lips fluttering as she stretches out her legs, stacking her shins on top of mine with an ease that makes me wish touching her was as uncomplicated as she makes it seem. "I'm going to have to fight back, aren't I? This isn't going to die down and go away."

"It might." I reach out, resting a hand on her knee because I can't resist the urge to touch her another second. "I'd say give it until Wednesday, talk to your agent when he's back on U.S. soil, and take it from there."

"Sounds like a plan," she says, voice breathier than it was before. But that might have something to do with the fact that my hand has slid up her knee to her thigh, my fingers curling until they press lightly into her bare skin. "Very...solid."

Oh, it's solid, all right.

It's hella firm and getting harder with every passing second.

"And what about you?" Her thighs part ever so slightly, making my mouth go dry.

"About me?" I echo, gaze locked on hers even as my traitorous hand slides higher, until my fingers brush the threads trailing from the bottom of her cutoff shorts.

"Is there anything you would like to discuss in the blanket fort of silence?" Her husky voice goes straight to my already-suffering cock. "Anything I can help you get off your chest? Aside from your shirt, of course? Though I'm happy to help you with that, too, if you'd like..."

My gaze narrows as my blood pressure spikes. "Guess 'friends' isn't going to work, huh?"

"Considering your hand is almost between my legs and all I can think about is biting your bottom lip, probably not," she says, before adding in a whisper that slays me, "You have the prettiest mouth, Valentine."

"Rafe," I grind out, fisting the edge of her shorts in my hand.

"No, in the blanket fort of silence, I'll call you Valentine." She arches her back, drawing my attention to her tight nipples, straining toward me beneath her shirt. "And you can call me Caroline. Different names for the different people we are here. People who are completely capable of keeping what happens here from causing trouble in the outside world."

I lean in, palm skimming up her hip to her waist as my mouth dips closer to hers. "Any coming in the blanket fort stays in the blanket fort?"

"Assuming you can make that happen." Her fingers thread into the hair at the nape of my neck. "I'll warn you up front, that's not always easy for me, and I'm not the kind of girl who's going to fake it to make you feel good about yourself."

"You won't have to fake anything, sweetheart." I brush my nose against hers, relishing this charged moment—the second before potential becomes reality, before I discover what this woman tastes like, what she feels like, the way she moves when she's pinned beneath me and desperate for the orgasm I'm about to deliver. "Just give me a number."

"A number." She exhales sharply as I cup her breast and sweep my thumb lightly over her nipple. "Number of what?"

"How many times do you want me to make you come?" My lips skim hers before I pull away, teasing her with the promise of a kiss and so much more.

Sparks flash in her eyes, issuing a challenge I can't wait to live up to. "Three, Valentine. You manage that, and you'll hold the record."

The words are the final blow to my self-control.

I avoid drama, but I never back down from a challenge. Especially one that involves making a beautiful woman come apart in my arms.

CHAPTER 6

RAFE

A second later my mouth is hot on hers, her arms are wrapped tight around my neck, and we're both moaning as I lie back, pulling her on top of me. Her thighs spread as she rocks her hips, grinding against where I'm already hard, my cock dying to be set free to do what he does best.

But he's going to have to stay locked and loaded a little longer.

If I'm going to deliver a holy trinity of orgasms, I need to keep my clothes on for the first two. It's been a while for me, and I'm not sure I'm going to be able to last more than fifteen, twenty minutes tops. I'm already so hot, my dick throbbing with the need to be buried deep inside the woman who's writhing on top of me, leaving no doubt she's going to rock my world the moment I glide inside her.

"Just how much heat are you packing, Valentine?"

Carrie asks, her words ending in a sharp intake of breath as I tug her tank top over her head, baring her gorgeous tits. "Feels like a serious situation down there."

"Nothing you can't handle, Caroline. Especially after you've come for me twice," I say, cupping her teacup-sized breasts in my palms as I roll her nipples between my fingers. "These are fucking beautiful, by the way."

"Thank you." She arches her back, moaning as I bend to kiss her breast, teasing my tongue over her taut flesh before sucking her nipple into my mouth. Her fingers curl into my hair, holding tight as I transfer my attention to her other nipple, which tilts up toward my mouth, practically begging to be ravished.

"This one is my favorite." I flick my tongue over the tight bud, relishing the salt and honey taste of her skin. "I like its style."

"I take it you noticed that they're crooked."

"They're individuals. With personality." I trace the pink circle of her areola, already knowing I'm never going to tire of worshiping her tits with my mouth.

But there is so much more delicious territory to explore, and so with a silent promise to get back to these beauties ASAP, I roll Carrie beneath me and kiss a trail from her chest to her navel.

I tease her belly button with my tongue, loving the way her stomach pulses beneath my mouth with its own heartbeat, a hungry throbbing that grows faster as I pop the button on her shorts and drag the zipper down with a slow, deliberate tug. She lifts her hips, silently giving me permission to keep going, an invitation I don't hesitate to accept.

I pull her shorts down her thighs, stripping them off and tossing them aside before settling between her legs to soak in the sight of the simple white cotton briefs that are the only thing keeping my mouth from her pussy.

"These are also sexy as hell." I run a finger beneath the elastic waist of the panties.

"You like granny panties?" she asks, biting her lip as she meets my gaze.

"Not as a general rule, but these do it for me." I run my hands up and down her thighs as I shift my attention to her mound, my balls aching as I inhale the scent of her arousal. She smells like honeysuckle wine, sweet but sharp and tangy, and I'm dying to get drunk on her. If we'd been together before, her panties would already be off and my tongue buried inside her, but this is the first time.

I want to savor this moment, these last few seconds before the big reveal, before I find out if her pussy is as adorable as the rest of her.

I lean in, pressing a kiss to her sex through the soft cotton, summoning a moan from low in Carrie's throat. "Do you want me to fuck you with my mouth, Caroline?" I ask, voice low.

"Oh, yes, Valentine," she says. "Please."

And because I'm not the kind to make a woman ask twice—at least not the first time we're together—I hook my thumbs in the sides of her panties and drag them down until I'm clear to push her thighs apart, settle into position, and claim my prize. And her pussy *is* a prize, so pink and slick and swollen it makes my chest ache at the carnal beauty of it.

"Incredible," I murmur, kissing her center, above her entrance, where all that flushed skin promises untold pleasures to any cock lucky enough to find its way inside her. Mine jerks hard in my jeans, demanding to be set free, but it's not time, not even close.

Ignoring the hunger building low in my body, making it feel like a lead weight is dragging between my legs, I settle in to make my offering, plead my case, to convince this sweet pussy to open for me and reveal all its secrets. Tilting my head, I fit my lips to her sex the way I would to her mouth and give her a French kiss I hope she'll never forget.

Judging by the way her breath speeds up and her thighs begin to tremble, the way her nails claw into my shoulders and her chest heaves, I know I'm on the right path. But I still don't expect the first to come so quickly. I've barely gotten started—haven't even sucked her clit into my mouth or bitten her in all the delicate places that secretly crave a bit of violence—when her hips lift up to my tongue and a shudder racks her body.

She cries out, a raw, abandoned sound that cuts right through me, making me groan against her slick skin as fresh heat coats my tongue, making me wild.

I surge over her, claiming her mouth with mine, stroking my tongue against hers, letting her taste how fucking incredible she is, how hot she makes me. "You're so sexy when you come," I murmur against her lips as I thrust two fingers into her pussy, desire spiraling higher as her inner walls clench around them.

"Oh my God," she whispers, arms trembling as she clings to my shoulders. "Yes, more. Please."

All too eager to oblige, I add a third finger. It's a tight fit, but she doesn't seem to mind. The added friction makes her moan, in fact, and when I glide my thumb over her clit, she shivers.

"No way," she breathes. "I can't do it again this soon. Can I?"

"Of course you can," I say, balls throbbing as I continue to fuck her with my hand. "You can do anything you set your mind to."

"But I... I..." She stiffens against me, coming with a sobbing sound as I bring the heel of my palm to her clit, grinding in circles, doing my best to draw her pleasure out for as long as possible. Her breath comes faster, faster and her entire body begins to quake as number two rockets right into number three.

When the third hits, she screams and the final thin thread of my self-control snaps. The sight of her abandoned to pleasure, the feel of her hot juices coating my fingers, the smell of her desire thick in the air—it's all too fucking much.

I reach for the close of my jeans and rip it open. But before I can get my zipper down or dispose of the hateful fabric keeping my cock from her incomparable pussy, Carrie makes a soft sniffling sound.

I look up to see tears streaming down her face and abandon my zipper like the tab is on fire.

"Hey, what's wrong?" I bring my shaking hand to her cheek, brushing the wetness from her flushed skin with my thumb.

"Nothing. That was amazing. Completely amazing." Her face crumples. "I don't know why I'm crying. Ignore me. I'm sorry."

I exhale with a shake of my head. "Of course I'm not going to ignore you. And don't be sorry. *I'm* sorry. I didn't mean to make you cry."

She blinks, sending fresh tears streaming over her thick lashes. "I know you didn't. You're so generous, and it was so easy for you to...to get me there. It made me..." She sniffs, clearly trying to regain control, but when she speaks, her voice shakes. "It made me realize that the men I've been with must not have tried very hard. Or maybe even tried at all."

My brows furrow as I stretch out beside her on the blanket, wincing as the movement makes the too-tight situation in my jeans even worse. "Maybe they were just shitty in bed."

Her lips press into a thin line. "All of them?"

"Or they were selfish pieces of shit," I say, placing a gentle hand on her stomach. "Either way, it isn't your fault."

She crosses her arms, concealing her lovely breasts from my gaze. "Isn't it? I mean, I picked them. And I don't know..." She swallows hard, her throat working. "I guess after all this shit with Jordan, the realization that my past lovers haven't considered my pleasure a priority hit harder than it usually would."

"If it's any consolation, I think a lot of men are selfish in bed," I say, hating to see her taking some dickhead's sub-par effort so personally. "Either because they don't know any better or because they were never taught that a woman's pleasure comes first, before you even *think* about taking yours. I had that drilled into my head from the time I was twelve. My dad took sex ed seriously."

Carrie's lips quirk. "So this isn't the first time you've heard that you're a superhero from the land of Orgasmia?"

My lips curve. "Well, no one's ever put it that way, but…"

She laughs as she lifts a hand, sweeping the last of the tears from her cheeks. "All right. I've got my shit together. Sorry about that." Her lips tremble into a smile. "So, where were we? I believe it was my turn to show you some appreciation."

I shake my head, even though my dick is still hard enough to crack walnuts and my balls are aching with the need for release.

But this doesn't feel right. She's saying the perfect words, but the look in her eyes says she's still too vulnerable, too exposed for me to feel certain I wouldn't be taking advantage somehow.

"Let's put that on hold for now." I sit up, grabbing her shirt and passing it back to her. "I don't know about you, but I'm starving. Want to grab subs? There's a great sandwich shop a few streets over."

It's actually eight long blocks over, but it's a nice day for a walk—and I'm going to need more than a few minutes to pull my shit together and stop thinking about how desperately I want to be inside her.

"Are you sure?" She frowns as she pulls her tank top on. "I'm not a selfish jerk, you know. I enjoy giving as well as receiving."

Her words send a graphic mental image of Carrie on her knees, running her pink tongue over the tip of my cock, rocketing through my head. A moment later I'm sweeping aside the sheet guarding the entrance to our fort and bolting into the air outside.

"I'm sure, it's cool," I call over my shoulder as I circle around the couch. "I just need to hit the restroom and I'll be ready to go."

As soon as I close the door to the bathroom behind me and lock it, I shove my jeans and boxer briefs down around my thighs and take my fever-hot dick in hand. I jerk off hard and fast, barreling toward release, fueled by the taste of Carrie's pussy still sweet in my mouth and fantasies of what it would have felt like to push inside her, to sink deep until every inch of my cock was gripped in her slick heat.

My hand tugs, slides, jerks, making fierce, urgent demands until I reach the pinnacle and spiral out. I come with a muffled groan, my release spilling hot over my own fingers, but the relief I was hoping for eludes me.

Yes, I've taken the edge off, but the hunger is still there, boiling in my bloodstream, assuring me I could be hard again in seconds if Carrie was spread out on my bed.

It's been a long time since I've wanted a woman like this. Which probably means I should abort this sandwich plan and take her home—do not spend the afternoon with her, do not take her back to the Land of Orgasmia, do not discover how incredible it feels to have her riding my cock, her violet eyes flashing as she comes with me buried deep inside her.

"Fuck that," I mutter as I wash my hands, already knowing I lack the will to follow that plan through. I've had a taste of the forbidden fruit, and now that I know how sweet it is, I only want more.

* * *

But by the time we grab sandwiches and get back to my place, Carrie looks totally beat, the kind of exhausted that takes hold of a person when they're stressed to the max. So instead of coaxing her back into our fort, I get her set up in the spare room for a nap.

When she wakes up, it's almost supper time, so I grill some pork chops on the balcony while she makes a salad and heats up potatoes, and we eat in front of the tiny television in the kitchen, watching *America's Funniest Home Videos* and making fun of each other for laughing. Afterward, we share some popcorn because she's apparently as much of a bottomless pit as I am and catch an old movie, but she's drooping again before Cary Grant catches the bad guys.

And so I give her a loaner toothbrush, assure her it's no big deal for her to crash here, and bid her good night with a friendly forehead kiss before retreating to my own room, where I jerk off again.

Because, apparently, I'm sixteen again.

But deep down, I know general horniness isn't the problem.

The problem is the irresistible woman in the other room, who's quickly getting beneath my skin.

CHAPTER 7

*From the texts of Carrie Haverford
and Emma Haverford Hunter*

Carrie: Just a heads up—I slept somewhere else last night, but I'll head back to the house to check on Mercy later today. I won't let Mom starve your baby while you're on your honeymoon, I promise. Hope you guys landed safe and are having a great time soaking up sun on the beach!

Emma: You slept somewhere else last night, huh?
I hope it was with a handsome devil who took your mind off your problems.

Carrie: Nah, just a cheap hotel.
I couldn't deal with Mom yesterday.
Needed a good night's sleep first.

Emma: I hear you. She doesn't handle public mortification very well, does she? Hers or anyone else's.

Carrie: That's the understatement of the century.

Emma: Ugh. I know. I'm sorry.
And I'm sorry we didn't get a chance to talk before
I left.

Carrie: Don't worry about it, Em. And don't apologize.
I'm the one who ghosted on your wedding breakfast.

Emma: It's okay. I spent half of it cleaning syrup off the baby, anyway. Which reminds me—don't worry about going home to check on Mercy if you would rather steer clear of Mom. I gave her a VERY stern talking to before we left. She's going to stick to the usual feeding schedule, she and Mercy will have a lovely long weekend together, and Dylan and I will be back to serve as Mom buffers on Tuesday. And as soon as we get back, you and I will powwow until we figure out what to do about Jordan and getting your career back on track.

Carrie: Thank you, but I'm a big girl, Em. I can handle my problems on my own.

Emma: Of course you can, but you don't have to handle them alone because you have family to help you. Dylan and I are both here for you, and if Mercy were old enough to understand the situation, I'm sure she would pour syrup all over Jordan's stupid head for you.

Carrie: I think Mercy considers a syrup bath a special treat, not a punishment, but I agree. And I would absolutely place my bets on her. For a thirteen-month-old, she's fierce.

Emma: She really is. And funny and sweet. I'm missing her a ridiculous amount already, and it's barely been a day. You don't think she's worried about us, do you? Wondering where Mommy and Daddy are and when we're coming back?
I want to call her, but Dylan keeps…distracting me.

Carrie: I bet he does. I think men are contractually obligated to distract their wives on their honeymoons. And I think you should stop worrying about Mercy and enjoy the distraction. She'll be fine. Mom was a lame Mom, but she's a great grandmother. I'm sure she's spoiling Mercy rotten and playing trains and ponies with her all day long and reading her a dozen stories before bed.

Emma: You're right, I'm
U
Wa
xoij

Carrie: Emma? You okay?

Five minutes later...

Carrie: Earth to Emma?

Six minutes later...

Carrie: Guess we got cut off. I'm pretty sure I only got part of your last message, so if it was something important shoot me an email or something. If it wasn't, then enjoy your honeymoon and we'll talk when you get home.
Have a blast, okay? Mercy is fine and so am I.

Three minutes later...

Emma: Sorry! Didn't mean to worry you. I got... distracted again.
It momentarily impaired my texting skills.

Carrie: Fourteen minutes, huh?
So, is that a quickie for you guys? Or are you at that stage in your relationship where fourteen minutes is considered a solid effort? Never mind, I don't want to know. Now that you're married, your sex life is gross and no longer up for discussion.

Emma: It is not gross! Not even a little bit.

Carrie: But it is. Marriage makes things gross. No offense...

Emma: None taken. I know your opinions on marriage, but I promise it doesn't have to be like Mom and Dad, Carrie. I'm so happy to be married to Dylan. Nothing has ever felt more right, and I know it's only going to get better with…

Hold on…

Plk

Carrie: Ew. You're getting "distracted" again, aren't you? Gag. Talk to you when you get back. Enjoy your honeymoon. And don't worry about anything here at home. It's under control.

CHAPTER 8

CARRIE

*N*othing is under control.

I'm decidedly *out* of control and on the verge of spiraling further into the Forbidden Zone. I came *this close* to banging my brother-in-law's brother yesterday, and if I remain in Rafe's company much longer, I have no doubt it's going to happen.

As we sit in his sunny breakfast nook, sipping coffee and flipping through the paper, it's a constant struggle to keep my focus on the words swimming in front of my eyes. Instead, I keep seeing the wicked curve of Rafe's mouth as he kissed his way up my thighs, feeling the silky texture of his hair as I clung to him for dear life while he made me feel things I haven't felt in years.

Yes, other guys have made me come, but none of the men I've been with recently have had Rafe's confidence, commitment, or undeniable skill.

Seriously, someone should award the man a master's degree in making out.

A PhD in doing the dirty deed.

A post-doctorate fellowship in the fine art of French kissing in the way the French surely intended, with a man's mouth making magic between his lover's legs until her bones melt and her mind explodes in a burst of pink champagne bubbles.

"Are you sure a granola bar is enough for you?" Rafe asks. "I could make oatmeal. Or I've got a melon in the fridge."

I clear my throat, forcing memories of his hands on my melons from my wayward thoughts. My breasts aren't nearly as big as melons, and this lust fog is unacceptable. I'm a grown woman, not a teenager who's just taken her first non-solo flight to Orgasm City, and it's time I start acting like it.

Especially considering what an emotional mess I was by the time we left the fort yesterday. It took me a nap, two meals, and a long, out-like-the-dead night's sleep to recover, for God's sake.

Calm, cool, and controlled are the words of the day, and I intend to embody them fully.

"Nah, I'm good, thanks." I casually flip to the business section. "I'm usually coffee only before ten a.m. It takes my stomach a few hours to wake up."

He grunts. "Not me. I wake up starving. Always."

I bite back a comment about that not being surprising, considering the calories he must have burned while he was medaling in the oral sex Olympics—triple gold, all the way—and push my half-eaten bar across the table. "Have the rest of mine. Seriously, I'm good. I run mostly on caffeine and rancor anyway. At least lately."

"The ill will I can understand, but you need more than caffeine." He nods toward me. "Eat your granola bar. It's the kind with extra protein, puts hair on your chest."

I arch a brow. "Hair on my chest hasn't been high on my wish list, but if after surveying the situation you think fuzz would be an improvement..."

He looks up, his dark eyes burning into mine over the top of his newspaper. "What happens in the blanket fort of silence stays in the blanket fort of silence."

My lips curve and awareness prickles across my skin. "Yes, sir. My apologies."

Rafe shakes his head in mock disapproval. "What am I going to do with you, Haverford?"

Race me to your bedroom and see which of us can get naked first?

Aloud I say, "Kick me to the curb, I suppose. I don't want to cramp your style. I'm sure you must have plans for this glorious Sunday."

He folds his paper in half and drops it onto the heavy wooden table. "I do, but you can tag along if you're looking for an excuse not to go home. I told Tristan I'd come help fix the paddock at the shelter where he works. They've got some horses coming in tomorrow. Shouldn't take me long, and you could help socialize the cats or something while you wait. Or dogs. Might be a ferret or two around. They've got all kinds of rescue animals up there."

"Nice of you to offer," I say, touched by the invitation. "But I can handle my mother solo until Emma gets back. You don't have to babysit me."

Rafe's lips curve. "Babysitting isn't what I had in mind."

I arch a brow, my pulse picking up. "No?"

"No," he says. "I was thinking we could go for a ride after, grab a bottle of wine, come back and drink it in the blanket fort of silence... I mean, we left it up. Might as well take advantage..."

"I did have an awfully nice time in that fort yesterday," I say, biting my lip. "But if we make a return visit, I don't want to be the only one taking her clothes off."

"I don't want that, either," he says, sending a sizzle racing across my skin. "I was thinking last night, while I was lying awake listening to you snore in the guest room..."

"I do not snore," I say calmly. "But continue."

His grin widens. "I was thinking that... Well, if what happens in secret, stays in secret, there's no reason for it not to happen again. Right?"

I press my tongue to the back of my teeth, forcing myself to think this through before leaping across the table and climbing into his lap. "We could never tell Dylan or Emma... Or do anything to make them suspect..."

"Absolutely," Rafe says soberly. "I think we've established that. We've also established that we're both adults, and both on the same page about what we want from each other."

"Hot sex, no strings," I supply, relishing the heat that flickers in his eyes.

"Yes. That." He holds my gaze with an intensity that makes my stomach flip as he adds in a huskier voice,

"Yesterday was incredible. But the next time we're together, I don't want to stop until I'm inside you."

Holy hell. Yes, please, and thank you.

I scoot my chair away from the table, ready to propose that bedroom race right now, but Rafe stops me with a hand lifted in the air. "Hold that thought. We'll get back to it ASAP, but we have to be in Healdsburg in forty minutes."

My lips turn down hard and my brow furrows in despair. He's got to be kidding me. Surely we can be ten minutes late to fix whatever he needs to fix and socialize the cats or whatever?

Rafe laughs. "You should see your face.'"

"I can feel my face." I stand, arms hanging limply at my sides. "It's the sad, confused face. The does-not-enjoy-waiting face."

"I don't enjoy waiting, either." He stands, circling the table, making my blood hotter with every step. "But I enjoy rushing even less." He draws me close until my breasts brush against his chest and a soft sound of longing escapes my lips. "I'm going to take my time with you, Haverford. It could take all day and all night."

"I don't have anywhere to be." I skim my palms up his arms to rest on his shoulders.

Damn, this man is well made—every inch of muscled flesh more tempting than the last—and I can't wait to make some memories worth keeping secret with him. But I have to be absolutely sure we're on that same page he was talking about.

"Just to be clear." I tip my head back, gazing up at him. "I'm not up for anything but the physical stuff from now on. I don't need or want to wade into the emotional shit anymore. I just want to feel good, to make *you* feel good, and to walk away without any regrets. I have enough of those already." I take a breath, hurrying on before he can speak. "And I wouldn't want to hurt you or disappoint you or do anything else to make your life unpleasant. You seem like a really decent guy, Valentine."

His mouth quirks up on one side. "Thank you, Caroline. I try to be a decent guy. And no worries. I haven't had a relationship that lasted longer than six months in my entire life, and I don't intend to start now."

My brows lift. "Shameless commitment-phobe?"

"Shameless serial monogamist," he corrects without a hint of self-consciousness, making me inclined to take him at his word. "And my only goal for our time together is for both of us to come hard and come often until it stops being entertaining to one or both parties. Then we go back to being friends who run into each other at the occasional family gathering. Easy. Simple."

"So you promise not to fall madly in love with me," I tease.

"I don't do love," he says seriously. "Not that kind, anyway. I'm not sure I'm capable, to be honest."

Brows lifting, I nod. "I'm not sure I am, either."

At least not anymore. After this nightmare with Jordan, I doubt I'll be able to trust a man enough to let love into the picture ever again. Not that I was anywhere close to being in love with Jordan, but I never imagined he'd become the sociopath currently plaguing my life.

It's enough to give a girl major trust issues.

"So we're good." Rafe's hand slides down to cup my bottom through my shorts, making my breath catch. "Now get your fine ass downstairs. The sooner we leave, the sooner we get back."

CHAPTER 9

RAFE

*R*oaring up the 101 North toward the privileged community of Healdsburg—with its quaint town square, obscenely wealthy citizenry, and abundance of passionate animal lovers who donate generously to my brother's non-profit—with Carrie's arms around my waist makes it hard to keep my mind off all the filthy things I want to do to her as soon as I've fulfilled my brotherly duties. But I do manage to clear my head enough to realize there's a flaw in my plan that I failed to notice when I was thinking with my dick.

Tristan knows me better than anyone else on earth.

Tristan also isn't blind, and he will realize immediately that there's something going on between Carrie and me.

And yeah, I could ask him to keep the situation on the down low—he's a vault, and I trust him with my life, let alone my secrets—but I don't want to burden my little brother with something he'll be obligated to keep from Dylan and Emma. Tris doesn't like secrets.

He's not a fan of lies, either, but what he doesn't know won't hurt him.

"You're looking for a cat," I murmur to Carrie after I've parked my bike and we're clipping our helmets to the handlebars. "Or a dog. An emotional support animal. That's why you asked to tag along with me today."

Carrie squints up at me, her eyes lighting with immediate understanding. "All right. But I don't actually have to leave with anything, do I? I love animals, don't get me wrong, but I'm living in a tiny cottage right now and my condo HOA in Berkeley doesn't allow pets."

"No, you don't have to leave with anything." I lead the way up the path, past the outer buildings that serve as the meeting rooms and food storage, toward the large main structure where the smaller animals are housed. "Just look interested and torn about making such a big decision. Maybe a little sad, too. Whatever it takes to keep Tristan from catching on to how desperate you are for me to fuck you."

She snorts. "Desperate, huh? I'm not the one with a semi, buddy."

"That's not a semi, I'm just hung like a horse," I say, fighting a smile.

"Care to duck behind one of those buildings and let me call your bluff?"

I laugh. I can't help it, though half of me thinks ducking behind an outbuilding is an excellent idea and the other half is ashamed of myself for having this much trouble getting my dick under control. "Fine," I mutter. "I'll cop to the semi if you'll admit your panties have been wet since you woke up this morning."

"So wet," she whispers as we near the main entrance. "In fact, I'm wet right now. Hot and wet and oh-so-ready..."

Instantly my semi swells to something much more serious, something that strains the front of my jeans and makes further progress into the shelter impossible. "You did that on purpose," I grit out as I grind to a halt beside the entrance, grateful that Sunday mornings are slow and there aren't any other people around to observe my inappropriate-for-the-animal-rescue situation.

She claps me chummily on the shoulder. "I did. I'm sorry."

"Sorry that you're not sorry is more like it."

Carrie laughs, a throaty chuckle that makes me want to bite her bare shoulder while I walk my fingers up her ribs, summoning more of that sexy sound from her lips. "Take a second to pull yourself together, Slick," she says. "I'll introduce myself to the lady at the front desk and express to her my deep, desperate need to acquire a sweet little pussycat to pet and stroke all day long."

"Evil woman," I force out through a clenched jaw.

More wicked laughter trails behind her as she disappears into the shelter.

But when I join her inside a few minutes later, her pretty face is pulled into a fretful expression as she flips through a binder showcasing the photos of pets available for adoption. "Thanks so much for letting me look," she says to a familiar freckled girl behind the counter. I vaguely remember meeting her a few months ago when I was here to help Tristan fix the transmission on one of the shelter's vans, but sadly her name didn't stick in my memory bank.

"Of course," Freckles says, smiling up at me before turning her attention back to Carrie. "Thanks for being understanding about our policies. The animals get so worked up when new people come in that we try to limit in-person pet browsing as much as possible. But if one of our buddies catches your eye, I can absolutely get you guys set up for a visit in one of the playrooms."

"I don't know how I'll ever choose," Carrie says. "They're all so adorable. Aw, look at this little guy!"

I glance over her shoulder, brows lifting. "Little? That dog's bigger than you are."

"Bear's about one hundred and eighty pounds of pure Saint Bernard," Freckles confirms. "And sheds and drools like it's his job. Super sweet guy, but probably not the best bet if you're living in a smaller space."

Carrie's nose wrinkles. "I am. Very small. Tiny, in fact."

She resumes flipping, and Freckles jabs a thumb over her shoulder. "Tristan's already out back pulling up the rotten fence posts, Rafe. Just head down the hall, all the way to the end, last door on the left."

"Thanks." I nod and start around the desk, leaving Freckles and Carrie discussing the barking tendencies of miniature pinchers vs. Chihuahuas, feeling awful that I can't remember the woman's name.

But I've always struggled with names, even with women I want to sleep with, and Freckles isn't my kind of girl. She's cute in a wholesome sort of way—glossy brown hair, pink cheeks, sparkly blue eyes—but she's obviously the sensitive sort, the kind who would get attached or hurt or both, and I don't mess with breakable people. I prefer women who are like me, with a thick skin and a sense of humor, who don't take life or love too seriously.

Women like the vixen leaning over the counter, granting me a heart-stopping glimpse down the front of her shirt as I pause at the end of the hall.

Damn, she's sexy. I can't remember the last time I was this eager to get a woman home, in my bed, under me and over me and—

Focus, man. Focus, finish, and head for home.

Determined to repair faster than I've ever repaired before, I push through the door and head toward the edge of the property.

Back here, the air is warmer than it is in front of the building, the morning sun already baking the exposed earth on the treeless hill. I find my brother at the far side of the paddock, surrounded by a pile of weathered old wood.

"Termites?" I kick an uprooted post that immediately cracks under the slight pressure.

"Or wood-boring beetles. Pain in my ass." Tristan runs a gloved hand over his short hair, making it stick up in spikes. Tristan and I are both the spitting image of our Italian mother—dark hair, dark eyes, and olive skin —but my brother is usually far more pulled together.

I'm the shaggy, scruffy before picture, and he's the polished, well-manicured after shot.

But today, in a pair of old jeans and a sweat-stained T-shirt with wood dust in his hair, Tristan is channeling his inner farm boy. Though, he looks skinnier than the last time we hooked up in Mercyville to throw together a shed for my dad, and his jaw is spotted with uneven stubble.

"You taking care of yourself, baby brother?" I ask, slapping him lightly on the shoulder. "Remembering to eat and sleep and shit like that?"

Tristan sighs. "You sound like Zoey. I'm fine."

Zoey. That's it. I pull up a mental image of Freckles and do my best to slap a label on it so I won't forget her name next time, then return my focus to my brother's face. "You don't look fine. You look tired and like you could use a burger. Maybe two."

He shakes his head. "The board decided we need a big summer fundraiser. In three weeks. And they still haven't found an event coordinator."

I grunt. "So, work stuff. Nothing to do with Kim?"

"Yes, work stuff," Tristan says, crouching down to pick up a freshly cut post. "Kim moved last week."

"Moved where?"

"Australia." Tristan jabs the stake into an empty hole in the earth. "She took an assistant winemaker job in Coonawarra, sold her car, and left. And if all goes well, she's never coming back."

"I'm sorry, man." I grab the bucket of pre-mixed concrete and fill in the hole around the post.

"Don't be sorry, just don't give me anything else to

worry about," Tristan says, voice dropping as he adds, "I saw you ride up with Carrie on the back of your bike. You two looked pretty chummy."

Inwardly, I curse myself for not taking the view from the back of the property into consideration. Outwardly, I shrug. "Just trying to cheer her up. She's pretty down about those pictures her ex leaked to the press. I thought a ride and some time with the animals would cheer her up."

"Just make sure the ride doesn't end in her pants."

"That doesn't even make sense," I say.

Tristan shoots me a hard look over the top of the post he's holding in place while the concrete sets.

"Fine." I lift my hands to my sides. "I promise, Carrie and I are just friends, and that's all we're ever going to be."

Friends, who sleep together, I add—silently, because I know better than to try to explain the situation to Tristan. As far as I know, Tris has only slept with one woman—Kim, his high school girlfriend and the one true love of his life.

Or at least she was the one true love until she told him she wanted to see other people and moved halfway around the world.

He's never experienced sex without emotion, and he certainly wouldn't believe me if I assured him that Carrie and I are a zero-risk proposition.

Better to tell a white lie and spare him the stress.

"Good," Tristan says after a beat, apparently satisfied. "Everything's solid with the family right now, and

I'd like for it to stay that way. And I don't want Carrie to get hurt, either. She's sweet."

A soft grunt of laughter escapes my throat before I can swallow it down.

"She is. Have you read her books?" he asks, a challenge in his voice.

"No, I don't read fiction. Especially kid fiction."

"Well, you should. You're missing some good stuff. And I think Carrie's stories would give you a window into who she really is." Tristan grabs another post from the freshly-cut pile. "I'm telling you, the tough girl act is just that—an act. She's sensitive, and I'm sure she's even more so after all the shit that's going down right now. So, either be her friend, or leave her alone. I don't want to be pissed at you. I'm already pissed off enough."

Ignoring the irritation sparking in my chest—I don't appreciate being painted as a womanizing monster, especially since I've always done my best to be good to the women I've been involved with—I nod. Tristan is going through a hard time himself, and he has a right to take his turn being a cranky bastard. Dylan and I have certainly done our share of grousing over the years while Tris remained the steady, thoughtful, even-handed brother.

"I hear you," I say. "And I'm glad you're pissed. That means you've moved on from feeling miserable and depressed, right?"

"Hell, I don't know." Tristan adjusts the post, making sure it's straight as I pour in the concrete. "I guess so. At least for today. It helps that it's already Monday where Kim is. We're not even living in the same day anymore.

She's in a future that's not my future, and I'm just... going to have to make the best of it."

"Want to go grab beers later? Maybe play some pool?" I ask, even as my libido howls in protest. It wants to spend quality naked time with Carrie in our blanket fort of silence, not hanging out with anyone with a dick. But Tristan is on my list of people I'll pass up getting laid for.

It's a short list—*very* short—but he's on it.

Thankfully, however, he shakes his head. "Thanks, but I've got to take Luke to the vet in town after we're done. He broke into Zoey's apartment above the exam room again and ate one of her socks."

I arch a brow. 'This is a common occurrence?"

"Sadly, yes," Tristan says. "He's got a hardcore dog crush on her, and it manifests in a compulsion to break into her place and eat her clothing. At least he didn't get her underwear this time. Last time, he got a pair of pink briefs. She was so mortified, poor thing. I've never seen someone blush that red. I was afraid she was going to quit and force me to hire three people to take her place. No way anyone else would get as much done as she does *and* agree to live on site so someone's always here in case of an emergency."

"Want me to take a look at the lock on her door while I'm here?" I ask, figuring I can spare the time since the paddock repair is going faster than I expected.

"That would be great. Thanks, man. I picked up a new lock at the hardware store this morning, but you'll be able to install it faster than I could."

We finish with the paddock, and while Tristan

cleans up, I head up to Zoey's and swap in the new lock, but I can already tell this is going to be a continuing problem. The mounting screws in the door jamb are too short. Until they're replaced, Luke is going to keep shoving his way inside and laying waste to Zoey's panty and sock collection. I make a note of the size screws I'll need to grab for a final fix and head back down to the main office to find Carrie behind the desk, flipping through a small mountain of paperwork.

"Don't tell me," I say, "you caved and adopted a Saint Bernard we're going to have to figure out how to get back to your place on a Harley built for two."

Carrie looks up with a distracted grin before squinting at something on the page in front of her. "No, I did something worse—I got a job."

"Carrie's going to coordinate the summer fundraiser," Tristan says, popping out from the office on the other side of the desk. "Thank you again for agreeing to help us out, Carrie. You're a lifesaver. I might actually be able to sleep a few hours tonight."

"My pleasure," she says, clicking a window closed on the computer. "And we shouldn't have any trouble pulling something together in three weeks. In my old job at the bookstore, I pulled off fundraisers in less time and we always had great turn outs, even without adorable animals to suck the public in. This will be even easier. I'll send Zoey a list of everything I need to build the web page tonight and get back to you tomorrow with a few options for event themes."

"Perfect," Tristan says, giving her a thumbs-up. "Zoey popped out to go grocery shopping, but I'm sure she'll get back to you quickly—she always does—and I'll send over your independent contractor paperwork tonight so we can make sure you get paid before the end of next week."

Carrie shakes her head. "No way, Tristan, I don't need—"

"We insist on paying you," he cuts in with a warm smile. "So don't even try to argue with me. We don't take advantage of people around here, especially family."

"Well, thank you." Carrie rises from the chair and gathers the stack of folders into her arms with a smile. "You Hunters are a generous group of people. No doubt about that."

Her tone is pure innocence, but her words are pointed enough that once we've said our goodbyes and are ambling down the path to the parking lot, I can't resist asking, "I agree the Hunters are generous as a rule, but I'm the most generous, right?"

She grins. "You were so generous yesterday that I've felt guilty all day."

"Ridiculous." I stop beside my bike, opening the saddlebag. "You shouldn't feel guilty. I enjoy being generous."

"But I do, too," she says, sliding her folder collection inside the bag and snapping it shut again. "I *love* it, in fact, so I insist on going first today."

"Going first?" I ask, though I have a pretty good idea what's on her mind.

"Going down first," she clarifies, sending a bolt of awareness surging between my legs. She steps closer, tilting her head back to hold my gaze as she adds, "I want you in my mouth, Valentine. I want to know what you taste like when you lose control."

"Rafe in public," I correct, but my heart isn't in it. My heart is in my throat and my balls are heavy and pulsing and my dick is trying out his Incredible Hulk impression, determined to burst through my jeans if that's what it takes to get to Carrie ASAP.

I'm dying to wrap an arm around her curvy body, pull her close, and devour her mouth with mine, giving her a taste of the way I intend to claim every inch of her as soon as we get back to my place. Instead—aware of the prying eyes that could be watching from the main building—I make *meaningful* eye contact.

Hot, intense, I'm-going-to-fuck-you-so-thoroughly-you'll-be-screaming-my-name-before-the-night-is-through eye contact and whisper, "Get your helmet on. Now."

"Why? Are we in a hurry?" she teases, but her voice is breathy and her nipples are hard beneath the thin cotton of her tank top.

Soon, they're going to be in my mouth and she's going to be squirming beneath me like she was last night, but this time I won't have to be a gentleman.

This time, I'll be able to keep going until we're both wasted on each other and feeling no pain. Not even a little bit.

CHAPTER 10

CARRIE

I can't remember the last time I was this turned on.

My entire body is hot, sensitized, alive in a way I haven't been for far too long. My blood is rushing, and my nerve endings are humming, and when the exit for downtown finally appears on the side of the 101, I'm so grateful I experience a full-body shudder of relief.

"Cold?" Rafe asks as we roll to a stop at the red light.

"No." I tighten my grip on his delicious body. "Just glad we're almost to your place."

"Me, too." He reaches back to squeeze my thigh, sending a fresh wave of longing rushing across my skin. "I can't wait to get you out of your clothes, Haverford."

"Ditto." I bite his tattooed shoulder through his T-shirt, eager to discover how much real estate that sexy ink takes up on his chest.

"Watch it, woman," he growls in response, fingers digging deeper into my thigh.

"Why? Don't you like biting?"

"I like it too much. Keep it up and I'm going to pull over and fuck you against the side of that building up there."

I consider calling his bluff and biting him again—just for the fun of making him growl—but then the light changes and the bike leaps forward, forcing me to hang on tight. The man is clearly in a hurry, and I'm not about to tell him to slow down.

Moments later, Rafe roars into the alley behind the shop and glides into one of two empty spaces behind his apartment. I slide off the back of his bike and rip off my helmet, ready to race him up to his place, but when I turn back to the historic brick building, I notice something I didn't before.

There, in the triangle of shade near the stairs, is a girl in tight black jeans, spike-heeled black boots, and a red tank top the same vibrant shade as her full red lips. Her silky black hair is pulled into a ponytailed adorned with a polka-dot scarf that lends her outfit a vintage feel, and her black bangs are a little too short, but the look works for her. With a face like a 1950s pinup girl and the boobs to match, she's completely easy on the eyes.

Though I'm guessing she wouldn't say the same about me. Her gaze sweeps critically up and down my cut-offs, tank top, and combat boots, lingering on my face for a long beat without looking me directly in the eye.

I'm about to introduce myself—simply to put an end to the awkward silence—when Rafe curses softly behind me and Pinup Girl's attention shifts his way, her dark eyes lighting up. "There you are! I was beginning to think you'd forgotten our date."

Their *date*.

Oh, dear…

Well, this is unpleasant. I don't have a jealous bone in my body—especially when it comes to fuck-buddies —but this girl's appearance on the scene is disappointing, to say the least. I was really, *really* looking forward to getting Rafe naked, which isn't going to be easy if he's out on a date with another woman.

Inside my chest, my heart sobs and flings itself dramatically onto my stomach while my pussy curls up into a neglected ball and weeps for what might have been. What might *never* be now that Rafe's been reminded that there are other hotter, sexier, less-complicated vaginas wandering around out there, eager to enjoy all the bounty that he has to give.

"I'm sorry, Alicia," Rafe says, moving in front of me to stake out neutral territory between his double bookings. "I did forget. I'm sorry. I totally spaced. I had to help my brother with a few things this afternoon and lost track of time."

"Oh, well, that's okay," she says with a resilient bounce of her shoulders. "I haven't been waiting long, and you're here now." Her gaze shifts uncomfortably my way before sliding to Rafe again. "I mean, unless you've got other plans…"

"Of course he doesn't," I say, waving a breezy hand. "I'm just his sister. I mean, technically his sister-*in-law's* *sister*, but same difference."

Rafe turns back, shooting me an unamused look that I answer with what I hope is a chill smile. If he wants to go with this girl, I don't want to stand in his way. Yes, I want him like I haven't wanted anyone in a long time, but I don't want him if he doesn't want me. I'm no one's pity fuck.

"We're just family," I insist.

"Oh, okay." Alicia's expression brightens as she holds out a hand and steps over several cracks in the asphalt to reach me. "I'm Alicia. Nice to meet you."

"Carrie." I take her slim, soft hand and give it a firm squeeze, a little sad to notice that she's even more stunning up close. And she smells like sugar and vanilla, a bit of a childlike scent, but far preferable to the smells I picked up from playing with semi-feral cats before jumping onto a Harley for a ride through the hot sun in clothes I've been wearing for going on two days.

Alicia's eyes narrow as she releases my palm. "Carrie. Why does that sound so familiar?"

I'm about to suggest that a good number of people are named Carrie—literally thousands in California alone—when her eyes go wide, and she lets out a squeal loud enough to make Rafe flinch.

"Carrie Haverford!" Alicia covers her smile with her hand, muffling her second shriek. "Oh my God, you look just like your picture! I grew up reading your books! Dude, I'm such a fan!"

"Grew up reading them, huh?" I ask sweetly as I arch a brow in Rafe's direction. I've only been published for six years. How old is this girl he's taking out for beers?

Is she even old enough to drink? To vote? To drive?

86

I'm about to ask Alicia if she's jailbait and save Rafe from himself, when she loops her arm through his and gives it a familiar squeeze, making me fear it might be too late.

"This is so cool, man," Alicia says. "I can't believe you're related to one of my favorite authors! We should all go out for beers, don't you think?" She stands on tiptoe, pressing a kiss to his cheek that sends a sour taste rushing through my mouth.

I'm *not* the jealous kind—I'm truly not—but that's *my* cheek. I was kissing it less than twenty-four hour ago. I should have dibs. At least until Rafe and I have a chance to bang the attraction seething between us out of our systems.

"I mean, we can go out just the two of us anytime," Alicia continues, wiggling her hips back and forth like a sexy puppy, "but how often is your sister in town?"

"Sister-in-law's sister," Rafe corrects with a stormy glance my way. "What do you say, Carrie? Do you want to go get beers with Alicia?"

His tone infers that he would rather be stripped naked, covered in honey, and tossed into a room filled with killer bees, but apparently, Alicia isn't great at reading subtext.

"Oh yes, please!" She bounces up and down, making her generous breasts bounce, too. "Please, please, please. You would make my day, my week, my life!"

And though I would also prefer some breed of exotic torture to drinking beers with the man I'm dying to get naked with and the girl he's probably going to get naked with later instead of me, I force a smile and say, "Sure."

There are few things in life that would compel me to step this far outside my comfort zone, but I've never been good at saying no to a fan. This girl read my books and they spoke to her. My brain took her brain on an adventure, and now we're connected by the bonds of holy pretend.

The least I can do is go for a beer with her, make small talk, and pretend I'm not desperate to jump on her date's penis, right?

"Fine," Rafe grinds out through a clenched jaw while Alicia continues to bounce happily and obliviously, proving she's probably a lot more fun in bed—and everywhere else—than I am. "Russian River Brewing company's just down the street. Might as well go someplace close."

I hear what he's left unspoken—*the sooner we get there, the sooner this hellish experience will be over*—loud and clear. But I choose to ignore his bad attitude.

After all, I'm not the one who forgot she had a date and double-booked her vagina. Alicia and I are both innocent parties here. So in the spirit of female solidarity, I hook my arm through hers as we start around the building to the alley leading onto the main street. "So, Alicia, tell me about yourself."

And she does—in detail.

So much detail, that by the time we reach the line of people waiting to get into Russian River Brewing Company I know that Alicia works as a wash girl at her sister's salon, is going to community college to get a degree in fashion design, loves Mexican food, playing bongo drums in her brother's band, and collecting miniature pig sculptures in equal measure, and has been in a book club since she was twelve years old.

"That's where I learned about your books," she says, squeezing my hand excitedly. "We'd just finished Harry Potter and my friend Theresa said I had to read *The Kingdom of Charm and Bone* next. I dove in and didn't come up for air until I'd finished the entire thing, and I legit cried when I found out the next book wasn't out yet. Those three months until book two came out were the longest of my entire life, I swear to God."

My brow furrows as I do the math and come up way short of twenty-one. "So, you're…eighteen?"

"Nineteen next week," she says, causing Rafe to stiffen beside her and cut a sharp glance her way. "But I've got a fake ID, no worries."

"You're eighteen?" he asks, horror and disbelief warring in his features.

I cough into the crook of my elbow, covering my laugh as Alicia turns to him.

"Of course I am, silly." She pats him on the arm. "I told you that."

"You most certainly did *not* tell me that." Rafe looks greener with every passing moment, a fact that gives me no small amount of joy. "I wouldn't have agreed to meet up for drinks today if I'd known that. My *nephews* are nineteen. I'm practically old enough to be your *father*."

Alicia laughs. "Oh, come on, you are not. Don't be silly."

Rafe scrubs a hand down his face. "I'm thirty-two."

She rolls her eyes. "Oh no! You're totally ancient, somebody call the nursing home." She giggles as she nudges my shoulder with hers. "Seriously, age is just a number. Right, Carrie?"

"Totally," I agree, fighting to keep the grin from my face as Rafe shifts his glare my way. "Unless you're trying to enlist in the military. Or vote. Or drink beer without a fake ID."

Rafe's eyes narrow dangerously as Alicia lifts a finger to her lips. "Right but keep that quiet. The bartender in here is a stickler. He took my friend Kayla's ID a few weeks ago, but she had an actual fake one with her picture on it. I just use my sister's old one. We look a lot alike, but she's three inches shorter so I always wear heels, just in case."

I'm still trying to make sense of that line of reasoning, when Rafe steps between us, putting one hand on Alicia's back and the other on mine, guiding us out of the line to get into the bar and down the sidewalk.

"What's up?" Alicia says, glancing over her shoulder. "The line's not that long."

"We're going to get coffee," Rafe says in a firm, dad-like voice that's oddly adorable. And sizzle-inducing, but then, just about everything he does has that effect upon me. "Or ice cream. Something without alcohol in it."

Alicia's nose wrinkles. "Oh, God, Rafe, please relax. You're being crazy."

"I'm not being crazy, I'm being responsible. I don't drink with people who aren't old enough to do it legally," he says, making me grin.

"I'm beginning to think this bad boy image of yours is all flash and no substance, Hunter." I reach over to pinch his waist, which of course has not a single ounce of fat between the muscle and his skin.

He glances my way, muttering for my ears only, "I'll prove you wrong as soon as this date from hell is over, Haverford."

"Seriously," Alicia agrees from his other side, oblivious to the wickedly sexy look he's shooting my way. "I thought you were cool."

"Nope," Rafe says. "I'm not cool." He shifts his attention Alicia's way. "So, I guess we're both okay with this being our first and only date?"

First and only date.

The words transform my grin into a relieved smile. He hasn't slept with this girl, he has no interest in sleeping with this girl, and as soon as we can find a place to suck down some coffee as quickly as possible, he's going to be mine. Mine all mine.

At least for the night.

"Yeah, I guess so." Alicia tilts her nose into the air, clearly not pleased with his response. But that's the way people are. We always want what we can't have. Now that Rafe's taken himself off the menu, I'm guessing Alicia will find him at least three times more appetizing than she did before.

Ten minutes later, as Alicia is sidling up to Rafe to get a lick of his salted caramel ice cream, her fascination with me forgotten in her attempts to get back in Rafe's good graces, my gut is proven correct yet again. Sometimes people are disappointingly predictable.

But not Rafe. He simply hands the rest of his cone over, thanks Alicia for her time, and circles around the table to rest a hand lightly on the small of my back. "Ready to get out of here, sis?" he asks in a wry tone.

"Past ready," I reply, wiggling my fingers at Alicia. "Nice meeting you."

"You, too," she says. "Can't wait for the next book!"

Before I can reply, Rafe has his arm around me, practically lifting me off my feet as he hustles us both toward the door. I settle for a, "Thanks so much!" tossed over my shoulder and then I'm outside, speed walking down the sidewalk next to a man who's clearly ready to get me home.

"In a hurry for some reason?" I tease.

"You. Me. No clothes. No third wheel. Sound good?"

"Sounds perfect," I say as we both break into a jog to clear the crosswalk in time. We hop the curb to safety with seconds to spare, but we don't slow our pace. We speed up until we're racing each other through downtown, grinning like we're up to no good.

Making quick work with his key, Rafe takes the stairs up to his place two at a time, with me not far behind. And when I reach the top, he's there to sweep me into his arms, making me even more breathless with a kiss.

CHAPTER 11

RAFE

*H*eart slamming against my ribs, I sweep Carrie into my arms and make a beeline for the blanket fort like we're both on fire and it's the only source of water for miles. I set her down just long enough to shove the sheet covering the entrance aside and then we both dive into the shadows, a tangle of arms and legs and lips coming together with bruising force as we tear at each other's clothes.

My shirt, her tank top, my boots, her bra—fabric flies as I do battle with the enemies keeping me from her velvet skin.

"Oh God, yes," she breathes as I jerk her shorts and panties sharply down her legs and tug her beneath me, finding her nipple with my teeth as my hand slides between her legs.

I groan against her sweet flesh as my fingers thrust into where she's so hot, so wet, so ready for me that I know I'm not going to be able to wait long. This entire afternoon has been foreplay—her breasts against my back as we rode, her thighs tight against mine, her eyes dancing as she raced me down the street—and I'm nearing my breaking point.

I need her. Now.

"Let me get a condom," I say, flicking my tongue across her other nipple. "I'll be back in thirty seconds."

"I'm on the pill." She tightens her grip on my hair. "And I'm clean. You?"

"Yes, but I need to get a condom anyway." I suck her tightness into my mouth, heart lurching as more wetness rushes over my fingers in response.

Fuck, she's so responsive. So hot and tight. I know it would feel incredible to glide inside her bare, but I can't take any chances.

"Because the Hunter men are baby making legends?" she asks, echoing my thoughts as she rakes her nails down my shoulders. "Don't worry. My pills can handle the Hunter swimmers. I just need you inside me, Valentine. You, not your hand." She arches into my mouth, cursing beneath her breath as I rake my teeth over the tip of her breast. "God, I feel like I'm going to die if you're not inside me in the next five seconds. You make me so crazy."

Crazy is the word for it.

It's crazy to take her like this, crazy to spread her thighs wide with a rough tug of my hands and drive my swollen length into her pussy to the hilt.

But I can't stop myself.

By the time I realize what I'm doing, I'm already inside her, pushing deep, a cry of relief bursting from my lips as she lifts her hips, welcoming me in, taking every inch until I'm completely sheathed inside her. Until I'm in heaven, nirvana, a state of consummate bliss so complete I have to suck in a breath and hold it, fighting the wave of pleasure that threatens to break me in half.

If I come in the first thrust like a fucking teenager experiencing pussy for the first time, I will never forgive myself, no matter how insanely tight she is or how incredible it feels to have her slick heat fisting me from root to tip.

I squeeze my eyes closed and reach down, gripping my dick tight at the base as I find her clit with my thumb.

"Yes, oh, yes, so good." Her spine arches, her tits lifting as I stroke her, tease her, focusing on getting her closer to the edge even as I talk myself away from the point of no return.

When I've reclaimed enough self-control to call myself a grown man again, I lengthen myself over her, claiming her lips as I cup her bottom in my hands.

"You're the best thing I've felt in ages," I breathe between kisses.

"Mind blowing." She hooks one leg around my hips, allowing me to glide even deeper, making my balls clench in appreciation. "Mind. Blown. All gone."

I groan in agreement as I rock faster, urging her closer at the end of each thrust, making sure I hit her sweet spot every time. I may not last long this first time, but I'm going to last long enough to feel her come.

"On top, woman," I murmur, nipping at her neck. "My hands need your tits."

"My tits need your hands," she says, moving with me as I roll to the side, reversing our position.

She lifts her arms, brushing her hair from her face, granting me the access I crave. I cup her breasts in my palms, rolling her tight nipples between my fingertips as she begins to roll her hips, riding me with her hands behind her head. She's so beautiful, so sexy, so shamelessly sensual as she rides me, taking me closer, closer, until I'm so close to losing myself inside her I can barely breathe.

Barely think.

All I can do is hold on as her thrusts grow urgent and the flush pinking her cheeks spreads until it reaches her chest and my worshiping hands. I pinch her nipples tighter in response, summoning a gasp from her parted lips. My balls are insanely heavy, dragging between my legs, demanding I come inside this woman, mark her as my territory, but I will not...

I *will* not...

I *will not* come until she—

"Yes! Oh God, yes!" Carrie's head falls back, and her hands cover mine, holding my palms to her breasts as she comes, her pussy locking down around me so hot and sweet I have no choice but to follow her over the edge.

I come with an animal sound, hands sliding down to grip her hips, pinning her to me as my cock pulses inside her, heaviness becoming weightlessness. I come so hard my vision blurs, and a muscle in my ass starts to twitch. So hard that I'm still clenching my jaw, riding out the final waves when Carrie collapses on top of me, her breath fast against my neck.

"I love you bare," she pants. "I love feeling you come inside me."

I make a sound low in my throat as I slip my hand between us, teasing her clit as I cup her ass in my free hand. "Again. You again."

"No way. I can't." But she doesn't fight me as I begin to rock her forward and back. "It's too soon."

"No, it's not." I rub her lightly at first, teasing the swollen flesh on either side of that powerful bundle of nerves, coaxing the subtler regions of her clit back to life.

When I learned the clitoris is like a tree, with hidden nerve endings reaching deeper into a woman's body, capable of layering in even more pleasure if a man knows what to do with them, I fell in love with clits all over again. The clitoris is the only organ in the human body devoted solely to giving pleasure. If that isn't evidence that women are miraculous and innately sexual creatures worthy of worship, I don't know what is.

And this woman is especially spectacular.

"I can feel you getting ready to go for me again," I murmur as she braces her arms on either side of my face, gazing down at me with a hooded look that makes me wish I were capable of recovering as fast as she can. "Relax. Let me take you there again, baby." I curl my middle finger, nudging my knuckle against her clit as my fingers continue to stroke her pussy on either side of where my dick is still buried inside of her.

"Let me watch you," I continue as she begins to rock faster, no longer needing my hand on her ass to urge her on. "Let me see how sexy you are when you come, Caroline. I want you to look right at me and lose control."

Her eyes widen and her lips part. Doubt flashes in her gaze, but then I see her make the choice to let me in, I hear the walls tumbling down as she comes, her gaze locked hard with mine. And I swear, in that moment, I feel her bliss wash through me, a wave of vibration that alters things inside me at a cellular level, transforming lust into something closer to addiction.

Fuck, but I want to feel that again.

And again.

This explosive connection that is so completely erotic that by the time Carrie stops trembling on top of me, my dick is back to half-mast.

And then she whispers, "I've never come that hard. Ever," and I'm rock-hard and ready to go again.

"I haven't even gotten started, Trouble," I promise. "I'm going to make it feel so good it hurts. I'm going to break you with orgasms."

"Oh yes," she sighs, lips curving against my chest. "Yes, please. Break me."

"Yes, ma'am," I promise, but this time I start slow and easy, taking her from behind with long, languid strokes, waiting until she's begging me for more before I fist my hand in her hair and fuck her like I mean it.

I take her hard, holding nothing back, and she takes

everything I have to give and more. We go until I lose count of how many times we've come together, until the sweet, salty smell of sex is thick under the blankets and I'm too tired to get up to get a drink of water, let alone take my usual pre-bed shower.

I'm about to suggest we brush teeth and crash in my bed when Carrie lets out a soft, but serious, snore.

I glance down to see her passed out on my chest, her eyes closed and her mouth parted softly in sleep, allowing more baby-bear-deep-in-hibernation sounds to escape her lips. With a tired smile, I drag a blanket over the top of us, shift a pillow under my head, and let sleep win this round, knowing the match was all ours.

Mine and Carrie's.

Someone should give us a fucking medal in fucking, I think, and then I'm out, counting orgasms instead of sheep.

CHAPTER 12

CARRIE

The morning sun warms my face, and my head is resting on something soft, but my hip aches and the rest of my bones are feeling creakier than usual. I open my eyes, squinting up at the ceiling. It's covered in flowers and way too close to my head, and for a long moment I have no idea where I am.

Then, in a blink, my synapses fire and memories come rushing in.

Memories of Rafe on top of me, me on top of Rafe, Rafe pinning my hands to the couch cushions as he drove into me from behind, making me come so hard I'm pretty sure I blacked out for a few minutes.

Or a few hours...

I don't remember what happened between collapsing post-fifth-or-tenth-orgasm and this morning, but apparently, we never made it out of the blanket fort, a fact that has my bones cursing me for sleeping on a hardwood floor covered only by a thinly padded quilt. Even more tragically, I'm alone, without the sexy man I was planning to wake with a good-morning blowjob.

I sit up, searching the fort for my clothes, intending to get dressed and go looking for my loaner toothbrush, Rafe, and coffee—in that order—but there's no sign of my shorts or shirt.

Or my panties...

"What the..." I pop the edge of my thumb into my mouth, nibbling as I try to remember where I started getting naked last night.

Before my sleep-deprived gray matter can pull up the necessary files, however, a deep voice sounds from the other side of the room.

"I put your clothes in the washer," Rafe says. "They should be ready to go into the dryer soon. I figured you would enjoy having something clean to wear."

"Are you a mind reader?" I start to wrap the sheet around myself, toga style, but stop when I hear footsteps headed my way.

"I am." A shadow falls across the sunny blankets and a moment later Rafe pulls the "door" to our fort aside. He's wearing nothing but boxer briefs and a smile, and I'm pretty sure I've never been as excited to see a mostly naked man in my life.

"You're not dressed," I say, grin stretching wider.

"You approve?" He crawls into the fort on his hands and knees, stalking me slowly, seductively, like the easy prey I am.

"I do. I like you better naked." I giggle as he crawls on top of me with a growl, but cover my mouth with my hand before his lips get any closer to mine. "Wait, I need to brush my teeth."

"No, you don't," he says, nuzzling his face into my neck.

"Yes, I do," I insist, moaning as he tugs the sheet lower, cupping my breast in his hand. "I have firm opinions about oral hygiene," I add, voice muffled by my fingers.

"I have firm opinions about fucking you. Right now." Rafe jerks the sheet from between us and settles between my legs, rocking the evidence of those convictions against my clit, swiftly eroding all my morning-breath beliefs.

"Two minutes. I'll be right back before you know I'm gone," I mutter weakly, but he's already shoving his boxer briefs down his thighs and teasing my entrance with his thickness, the head of his cock so hot I can't bear to wait another second.

I need that heat inside me, making me burn the way no one ever has before. So I spread my legs wider and lift my hips, silently welcoming him in.

"Fuck, Carrie." Rafe groans as he sinks into where I'm already wet and oh-so-ready, simply from spending a few moments in his erotically charged presence.

"Yes." I dig my fingers into the thick muscles of his ass, pulling him closer, deeper, until he fills me completely. "Oh, yes, right there."

"God, Trouble, you feel so good." He pulls out and glides back in again, stroking between my legs as I rock into him, matching his pace. "I dreamt about this all night. About how perfect you are. How you were made for me to fuck you."

"So that's my destiny?" I ask, already breathless. "I wondered if I had one."

"You do. And this is it." His hands slide beneath my bottom, pulling me closer at the end of his next thrust, sending a shockwave of bliss coursing through me as his body grinds against my clit. "Just like this."

"Oh yes, like that." I cling to his shoulders, my pulse racing faster. "Just like that. Don't stop, please, don't stop."

"I'm not going to stop," he promises, fingers threading through mine, pinning my right hand to the floor above my head. "Not until you come for me. I need to feel you come on my cock, Caroline. I want your pussy dripping before I come inside you."

I arch closer, relishing the way the crisp hairs on his chest brush my sensitized nipples as I climb closer, closer... "I love it when you come in me," I breathe. "I love watching you lose control."

Rafe groans, the need in the sound making my blood pressure spike even before he begins driving deeper, harder, the hand beneath my ass keeping my pelvis tilted so that every stroke gives my clit exactly what she needs. What *I* need. What I'm so desperate for even after having this man half a dozen times last night.

God, I don't know if I'm ever going to get enough of him.

It's a scary thought, but I'm too far gone to be afraid of anything. I'm so close, the tension fisting low in my body twisting tighter, tighter, until the pressure reaches critical mass.

I come with the force of a star being devoured by its own gravity as Rafe calls out my name, making more of those sexy animal sounds that assure me he's falling right along with me. Falling, flying, shattering into a million particles of stardust that sparkle away into the darkness of space, reflecting light wherever they go.

I wrap my arms tight around him as we continue to rock together, bodies slick and hot, riding the wave until we're both limp and wasted, lying boneless on the floor.

But unfortunately not *literally* boneless, or my tail-bone wouldn't be aching like someone's been using it as a punching bag.

"I truly loved being pinned beneath you, Slick, but I need to get up," I whisper, pressing a kiss to his neck as I skim my fingers up and down the valley of his spine. "Before my tailbone breaks in half on this hard-ass floor."

"Shit. Sorry." Rafe shifts, lifting his body off of mine, sadly taking his cock with him as he moves.

I hate to feel it go, but I take comfort in knowing I'm going to make friends with it again very soon. Rafe and I are averaging about every hour and a half at this point, a pace that is completely unsustainable, but which I intend to enjoy for as long as it lasts.

He stretches out beside me, brushing my tangled hair from my forehead with a guilty grin. "You okay? I didn't mean to break you."

"You didn't, I'm fine." I stretch, wincing as I discover

more aches and pains. "But I think if fucking you really were my one true purpose, my body wouldn't be as sore as it is right now."

"Not true." Rafe shakes his head as he reaches for his discarded boxers. "We just need to get your body on something soft as well as under something hard. From now on, we're fucking in my bed."

I arch a brow. "Doesn't that violate the blanket fort of silence terms of service?"

"This entire apartment is now annexed into the fort, and we're not leaving it for twenty-four hours. It's my last day of staycation, and I intend to make the most of it by keeping you out of your clothes as much as possible."

"You're off to an excellent start," I say, with a smile. "And that sounds perfect."

"Good." He rubs his hands together, a devilish grin on his face that makes me laugh. "I've already put in an order for groceries so we won't have to worry about going out for food. They're going to be delivered in about an hour, which gives us just enough time for me to give you a tailbone rub in the shower. If we hurry."

"An hour-long tailbone rub?" I shift onto my knees and wrap the sheet around me, tucking it into place above my breasts. "That's a generous offer."

"I'm a generous man." He leans in, kissing my cheek before whispering in my ear, "But I confess I'm planning to rub other parts of you while we're in there."

"Oh, I would hope so." I loop my arms around his neck, tilting my head back as he kisses his way down my throat. "All the parts, please."

"Every inch," he promises.

And he does, every single centimeter, proving he's a man of his word.

As I come for the second time this morning, with Rafe's body hot against my back and the cool tile pressed to my front and steamy water filling the air, I wish I could bottle these memories. I want to distill each one into a perfume I can spritz on for special occasions, mold them into bath bombs I can soak in for hours when I'm back in Berkeley feeling lonely and wondering if I'll ever be this effortlessly connected to another person again.

But memories are slippery creatures. The harder we try to pin them down, bottle them up, carve them into stone, the faster they slide through our fingers.

So I give up on committing every second to memory and let myself get lost in Rafe and all the extraordinary things he makes me feel. This moment may be lost to me someday, but for now, it and this incredible man are all mine.

CHAPTER 13

SIX DAYS LATER...

From the texts of Carrie Haverford and Rafe Hunter

Rafe: Just closed the shop and I'm headed out the door.
ETA six-thirty.
Should I pick you up by the berry farm or the cider
place?

Carrie: Behind the Murphy bed workshop down the
street from the cider place. I think we need to mix it up.
The same people walk the trail every evening, and some
of them are starting to give me side-eye. They're either
wondering what I'm doing loitering around the same
spots every night, or they've seen the pictures.
Maybe both.

Rafe: Any progress on that front? Are the police going
to have enough to charge that piece of shit with a
misdemeanor?

Carrie: We're still not sure, but threatening Jordan with legal action has sent him scurrying back into his troll lair, and my new publicist is doing her best to change the conversation. So far, so good, and none of the schools I booked for the fall have cancelled yet, so...

Rafe: That bodes well.

Carrie: It does. Now I just have to wait for the stink to blow over.
In the meantime, I've been trying to get as much work done as possible.
Though I confess that daydreaming about last night in the waterfall made writing a children's book with no sex in it difficult today...

Rafe: Fuck... I've been thinking about it all day, too.
The water streaming over your skin...
The way you were shivering until I warmed you up with my mouth...

Carrie: Stop! I'm already walking to the pickup point.
If you get me worked up, there's nothing I can do about it.

Rafe: That reminds me, I'd like to watch you get yourself off.
Can we put that on our fuck-genda?
Your fingers between your legs while I play with your nipples?

Carrie: You're a bad, bad man.

Rafe: I'm not bad. I'm good.
And I'm going to prove it to you tonight, Haverford.
I borrowed my friend Cal's car.
It's a 1959 Cadillac Eldorado with a massive back seat.

Carrie: Ooo… Are we going parking?! Like teenagers?
Will you get me home before curfew?

Rafe: That's a hard no on the curfew.
I'm not time's bitch or anyone else's, baby.

Carrie: LOL. And yet you're always on time to pick
me up…

Rafe: I won't be if you don't stop texting me, so I can get
in the car.

Carrie: Done. Get in the car. I want you here ten
minutes ago.

Rafe: Me, too. See you soon, Trouble.

Carrie: Can't wait.

CHAPTER 14

RAFE

"**C**an I look now?" Carrie's knees tap together as I pull off onto the gravel road leading to our final destination, drawing my attention to her thighs and all that soft, creamy skin I can't wait to get my mouth on as soon as I get her out of her shorts.

"Not yet," I say, slowing to keep the wheels from kicking dust into the car. "The surprise is better if you don't see it coming."

She growls softly. "You're killing me, Hunter. I don't like surprises. I really don't."

"You're going to like this one, so keep 'em closed. We're almost there." Guiding the Cadillac around piles of old furniture, plywood, clothes mildewing in weathered garbage bags, and the rest of the trash that makes the Tate place look like something from an episode of *Hoarders Take on the Great Outdoors*, I shift into low gear to make the climb up the hill at the back of the property.

The Tates were an odd crew, but their tendency to collect strange shit is what makes this place so special. It's a gorgeous slice of land, ten acres that would be ideal for a hobby farm or a boutique hotel. But so far no one's put in a bid. The property's been for sale for years, since the last Tate sister passed, and it's going to take someone with imagination to see past the cleanup that needs to be done.

And the general creepiness, I think as we hit the top of the hill and pull past a row of carousel horses stuck into the ground on the side of the drive.

They're from several different carousels, and the mismatched bodies and varying degrees of rot send spiders crawling up my spine every time. Even more than the trash heaps, the horses are why I want Carrie's eyes covered until we get to the cool part of the surprise.

Better if she doesn't see what we had to go through to get there until after the fun has been had.

"What's that smell?" Carrie lifts her nose into the air.

"Old logs," I say, figuring it's not really a lie. The rotten horses were all logs at one point or another.

"Smells like my grandmother's house," Carrie says. "Her roof leaked all the time. One time I found moss growing on the legs of her coffee table."

"We'll be past it soon." I turn right, heading toward the clearing at the back of the property.

"And you promise you're not driving me out in the middle of the woods so no one will hear me scream while you carve out my kidneys for your kidney collection?"

I smile. "I don't have a kidney collection."

"You're a liver man? Lungs? Pancreas? Don't say intestines, because that's just disgusting."

I reach over, squeezing her thigh. "I have no designs on your organs, just all the skin holding them together."

"That's what they all say."

I laugh as I pull into a parking spot in the middle of the field and cut the engine. "Open your eyes, woman. We're here."

Her hands fall to her lap as she blinks fast, her lips parting with a soft gasp as she gets her first glimpse of the giant screen surrounded by redwoods. The trees block the light from the setting sun but allow enough rosy glow through the limbs to make the Tate's private drive-in feel like something from a fairy tale.

"Oh, Rafe... It's incredible." Carrie turns, taking in the rest of our surroundings. "Where are we? Why isn't anyone else here?"

"Technically we're not supposed to be here, either," I confess. "The Tates used to let my brothers and me come watch movies whenever we wanted, but they've all passed away and the property is up for sale." I hold up my keys. "But I've still got the key to the movie shed, and I know how to load the projector."

Her smile is delighted—bright, beautiful, and as unfazed by the fact that we're trespassing as I'd hoped it would be. "Can I help? I've never seen a projector up close before. I want to know how it works."

"Sure, come on back." I swing out of the car and start around to her door, but she's already out, bounding through the tall grass pushing up from the gravel covering the clearing to grab hold of my hand.

"Come on." She tugs me faster toward the red shed at the back of the rows of speakers. "This is not the time for the sexy swagger. You have to learn to walk faster sometimes, like when exciting things are happening."

I laugh. "I don't get in a hurry, Haverford. And we have to wait at least thirty minutes for it to be dark enough to start the show, anyway."

"Not if we pick something we've seen. Our memories will fill in the blurry parts."

"Picking something we've seen is probably a given," I admit. "The Tate's collection is mostly old horror flicks and every movie ever made about Vietnam, with a few random cartoons and things thrown into the mix."

Carrie slows and some of the excitement fades from her expression. "Oh. Well, maybe a cartoon, then? If that's okay? War movies make me sad, and I confess I'm a huge baby who is terrified by anything scary."

I squeeze her fingers with a grin. "Does that mean you'll be crawling into my lap, begging me to protect you from the chainsaw murderer?"

She snorts. "It means I'll be wetting my pants in your friend's car. Seriously, I'll have nightmares for weeks if I watch people getting murdered in the middle of the woods while we're at an abandoned drive-in movie theater in the middle of the woods. My imagination is way too hyperactive to let that slide."

"I hear you." I release her hand as we reach the shed and fit the key into the lock. "There are a couple raunchy eighties comedies in the mix, too. But if we can't find them, we'll watch a cartoon. They've got *Snow White and the Seven Dwarfs* and 'Heigh-Ho' is a pretty kick ass make out song you know, when you think about it."

"You calling me a ho, mister?" She starts to step past me into the musty interior, but I wrap my arm around her waist, pulling her close.

"Never." I lean down, brushing my lips softly against hers as I whisper, "But I definitely want you naked in the backseat after the stars come out. I want to fuck you with moonlight in your hair."

"That sounds lovely." She presses onto tiptoe to deepen the kiss, breath hitching as my hand finds its way up her T-shirt to cup her breast. "But maybe we could do a warmup session, first? Just to hold us over until it's dark?"

"I think that can be arranged." I roll her nipple between my fingers as I simultaneously pop the button at the top of her shorts. A moment later, my hand is down the front of her panties and my fingers are pushing inside where she's wet. And fuck, but it drives me crazy to feel how ready she is for me, to know she's spent the ride here wanting me as much as I want her.

"I need to be inside you ten minutes ago, Trouble," I breathe against her lips as she works open my belt with shaking hands.

"Yes, please," she says, as I jerk her shorts down over her ass. The material skims her legs as it falls to the ground, and then I lift her into my arms, urging her legs around me. I shove my jeans and boxers down far enough to free my cock and then she's there, slick and hot, sinking down onto my suffering length.

But the moment I'm buried inside her, I suffer no more. Bliss sharpened by anticipation cuts through me, severing my ties to everything but this moment, this woman, this pleasure pulsing hot and fast through my veins.

"Jesus, I missed you." She clings to my shoulders as I spin us both, leaning her against the wall of the shed, allowing each thrust to glide deeper into the only place my cock wants to be. "Twenty-four hours is too long."

"Way too long," I agree, groaning as she drags her teeth across my jaw. "You should come stay with me until you're ready to go back to the city."

"I can't. We'd get caught." She rocks into me with sharper rolls of her hips, showing me how she wants it. And I am, as always, happy to oblige.

"No, we wouldn't." I grip her ass tight in my hands, grinding deep, loving the way she trembles in response.

"Yes, we—" She breaks off with a moan. "Damn Rafe, I'm already so close."

"Me, too. God, baby, you drive me crazy."

"Yes," she gasps, fresh heat rushing from her body to coat my cock, easing my way, giving me the freedom to fuck her harder, faster, until our bodies are slamming together and the sounds of skin against skin and breath coming fast are the only thing I can hear over the thunder of my heart.

And then Carrie cries out, nails digging into the skin at the back of my neck as she comes, her pussy gripping me tight, refusing to let me go until I answer her pleasure with my own. With a shudder, I let the reins slip through my fingers, surrendering to the wave that sweeps through my body, leveling me with its intensity, its beauty.

Beauty isn't a word that usually pops into my head during sex, but it's true.

It's beautiful with her, so easy and simple and honest. There's no guilt or worry, no shame, there's just this woman who throws open the doors to her self and puts her pleasure in my hands, holding nothing back.

"Damn, Trouble," I murmur against the damp skin at her neck, eyes squeezed closed as the last tremors pulse through me. "You're ruining me for other pussy."

"It's so good," she agrees, brushing my hair from my face as she grins up at me. "But you'll eventually recover. Even chocolate cake gets old after a while."

"I hate chocolate cake."

"What?" Her swollen lips form a scandalized O that makes me want to kiss her again. So I do, even as she protests between kisses that chocolate cake is the best thing that ever happened to mankind.

"Aside from cupcakes." She leans her head back as I kiss my way down her neck. "Because cupcakes have all the fun of cake, but with a higher cake-to-icing ratio."

"Not into sweet things. Except your pussy." I curse softly beneath my breath. "So, I'm pretty pissed at myself for sperming it up in there and ruining it for my mouth for the rest of the night."

She laughs. "Oh my God. Put me down."

"What's wrong?" I ask as she laughs harder. "What?"

"Sperming it up." She squirms out of my arms and

reaches for her discarded shorts. "Seriously, what's wrong with you? How are you the reigning Sex King of Sonoma County when you say stuff like that?"

I shrug, grinning as I adjust my clothes. "Standards are low around here?"

"I don't think that's it." She shakes her head, eyes sparkling. "I think it's your magical cock making up for your ridiculous mouth."

"My mouth is not ridiculous. And I'll prove it as soon as I get you back to my place for a shower tonight." I draw her back into my arms because ten seconds after I've come, I start craving her body again. She's an addiction, this woman.

"We can't." Her palms brush back and forth across my chest. "You said yourself—you never know when Dylan's coming in to work. As early as he gets up, he could be downstairs making beer before I have a chance to sneak out."

"Then I'll carry you out in my suitcase. You're small. You'll fit."

She rolls her eyes. "No, I won't. And my mom is watching my every move, too. She's just looking for a reason to lecture me lately, and I don't want to give her one by staying out all night again."

"All right." I sigh, reluctantly abandoning my shower plans. "As long as you'll ride my magical cock in the back seat while I bite your nipples."

Carrie's teeth dig into her bottom lip as she shakes her head.

"Is that a no?"

"No," she says softly. "That's me wondering how you

can make me want you again when I just came so hard I still can't feel my toes."

Dropping my hands to cup her ass, I lean close and whisper, "Because I'm ruining you, too. You're hooked on my cock, Trouble. Admit it."

She grins, raking her nails over my swelling length through my jeans. "Fine, I admit it. So what should we do about this mutual addiction? You think we need a twelve-step program?"

I shake my head. "No, we need twelve days alone on a beach with nothing to do but each other. I could get away in August. Maybe sooner if I get Cal to watch the shop. You up for a sex-cation? We could rent a house on the beach in Mexico, see if we can set a world orgasm record?"

"Sounds tempting," she says even as she steps out of my arms, the tension creeping into her features making it clear I've said the wrong thing. "But I can't really commit to anything in the future. I'm not in that head-space right now."

"It's just sex, Carrie," I say, lips curving. "I'm not asking you to be my steady date. I'm asking you to let me make you feel good in between relaxing on the beach and drinking beer with fresh lime in it. You could use some downtime."

"I could." Her hands slip into her pockets as her gaze falls to the ground. "I'm just not sure where I'll be with work and the scandal and everything else by then. I might be filing a lawsuit against the last guy I went to the beach with, you know? Doesn't seem like the best time to head off to the beach with someone else. Especially someone I'm supposed to be keeping things low key with."

I nod, fighting not to let my disappointment show. It's bad enough that I'm so bummed that she turned me down. It would be even worse if she knew it. Instead, I smile and nod toward the increasingly shadowy interior of the shed. "I hear you. No big deal. But we should probably pick a movie. It's almost dark enough to start something."

She grins, clearly relieved. "Oh, good. I'm excited. I've never been to a drive-in."

"Drive-in virgin, huh?" I tease as I step around her. "Don't worry, I won't be gentle."

"I would hope not," she quips.

I slap her ass, making her laugh as we flip on the lights and open the metal locker holding the Tate film collection. We find a copy of *Sixteen Candles* at the back of the locker, behind *Good Morning Vietnam* and *Full Metal Jacket*, and settle in for some light-hearted teen angst.

We've barely made it past the first fifteen minutes, however, before we're all over each other again, tumbling into the backseat as the movie flickers in the background.

As promised, Carrie straddles me, riding me as I suck and bite her nipples, giving me exactly what I want from her—hot sex with no strings.

She's right. It's better this way. Just her and me and this moment, without a past or a future or anything to interfere with how simple and perfect this pleasure is.

But when I drop her off at the edge of the vineyard

later, so she can sneak into her tiny cottage unobserved, I can't help wishing I was going with her.

Or that she was coming with me.

Wanting more time doesn't mean I want feelings or the future. Wanting more time just means I want to wake up with her in my bed so we can start the day off as nature intended—with an orgasm or two—and have sex in a hammock on the beach.

I just need to find a better way to pose the question, a way that won't scare off my commitment-phobic sex kitten. Luckily for me, as a long-standing commitment-avoider myself, I know where she's coming from.

By the time I get home, I already have a few ideas simmering.

I'm going to have Carrie in my bed again. Oh yes, I will...

It's just a matter of time...

CHAPTER 15

CARRIE

Three days later...

*F*or the first time since Rafe and I started our Bang-a-Pa-Looza, he has to work late, so I rearrange my schedule to make sure I'm out accomplishing things instead of sitting alone in the cottage, listening to my vagina softly weep.

Because my vagina is ridiculous and spoiled rotten and has nothing at all to cry about. At least not right now. When I go back to Berkeley and my fuck buddy is no longer an easy fifteen-minute trip across town, and I have to go weeks or even months without Rafe's penis in my life, that will be a different story.

But I won't think about that now.

I *can't* think about it.

I have enough on my plate between navigating my P.R. nightmares, finishing a book that's due in October, and pulling together a Yappy Hour wine, beer, and puppy-treat fundraiser eighteen days from now.

I should have had these fliers printed and posted two days ago. And if I were a smart organizer, determined to use her time wisely, I would text Zoey, get her and Tristan's thoughts via email, and move forward with the printing without wasting time driving all the way out to the shelter.

But the shelter is my only semi-reasonable excuse to leave the cottage, so I print out my flier designs in Emma's office and prepare to make my escape before family dinner commences. Emma always offers to include me, but I don't want to impose upon her newly-married life more than once or twice a week, especially not on nights when my mother has been sitting for Mercy and joins them for the evening meal. If we were being honest, I think Mom and I would both admit that we need more time apart than we've been getting, but I also have no doubt that Renee will lay on a guilt trip for skipping family bonding time if she catches me on my way out.

Stealth is of the utmost importance…

On kitty-cat silent feet, I sneak out of Emma's office and through the living room with the fliers tucked under one arm and my purse slung over the other. The door to Mercy's room remains closed, and not a peep comes from the other side of the house, making me think my mom might be taking a nap, too.

Score!

I'm out the door, the Mini Monster in sight and my keys in hand, when a voice from the rocking chair on the porch announces, "You shouldn't be exhausting yourself with charity work right now, Carrie," making me jump and drop everything, sending my purse thudding onto the porch and fliers scattering across the planks.

"Jesus, Mom, you scared me!" I turn to see Renee camped out in the red rocker. My niece coos happily on her lap, deeply engrossed in chewing on her stuffed fox's oversized ear. "Why are you lurking out here when it's a hundred degrees outside? You and Mercy should be inside in the air conditioning."

"It's perfectly nice in the shade," Mom says with a sniff. "And Mercy and I like to have our afternoon treat on the porch so we can watch Mama come home."

"Mama!" Mercy pipes up with a smile, pointing a pudgy finger toward the vineyard where my sister is busy supervising the thinning of the fruit.

I smile and nod. "She'll be home soon. You love your mama, huh?"

Mercy kicks her legs and lets out a delighted squeal that breaks my heart a little.

What must it be like to be Emma? To know that just coming home from work is going to thrill the daylights out of this adorable person waiting for her? I've always had a soft spot for babies, but it wasn't until I became an aunt that I started to seriously consider motherhood as part of my long-term plan. Seeing the incredible bond between Emma and Mercy, and how sweet that mama love is, makes me want it for myself someday.

"Dogs and cats are great if you've got time to spare," my mother continues, reminding me that mother-daughter bonds aren't always rosy and sweet. "But they're not going to pay your bills." She ducks her head, cooing in a high-pitched voice as she tickles my niece's belly, "Isn't that right, Mercy? Aunty Carrie needs to figure out her Plan B, not work for free."

"I'm not working for free," I say, raising my voice to be heard over Mercy's squeal of laughter. "I'm getting paid to coordinate the fundraiser for the shelter. And I don't need a Plan B. I'm under contract for two more books and sales of the first books in the series are still strong."

"That's not what I heard," my mom says, still in her baby voice though she's clearly talking to me, not Mercy. "Emma told me your agent said sales were down and he wants you to work on a thriller under another pen name."

Jaw clenching, I silently curse my sister's loose lips. Though, honestly, my mom could wring gossip out of a turnip. She's *that* good at ferreting out things she's not supposed to know.

"It's fine." I stoop down to gather the fliers from the porch. "Down doesn't mean they aren't still solid, and Seth suggested the thriller because I asked him about writing for adults and where he thought I might find an audience. It was about expanding and trying new things, not abandoning what's already working."

Renee's lips prune in a silently dubious display, making Mercy laugh. She reaches for her grandma's mouth, doing her best to pull the lips from Renee's face and making my mother's next words impossible to understand.

Thank goodness for those sweet, grabby little fingers.

"Can't hear you, Mom, gotta go," I call over my shoulder as I jog down the stairs to my car.

Thankfully the Mini Monster starts on the first try, and I'm rumbling across the gravel and up the lane before Renee regains control of her mouth.

I know Emma's happy that Mom has committed to babysitting three afternoons a week so Mercy doesn't have to go to daycare, but I can't help wishing my mother's generosity of spirit had stayed offline for a few more weeks. All the quality time with her has my jaw perpetually clenched and my shoulders full of stress knots.

Even with my nightly escapes with Rafe and my mornings spent in self-imposed isolation—writing as fast as I can before the tiny house heats to an insufferable level of stuffiness—I'm seeing way more of her than I would like to, bringing back memories I've done my best to avoid pulling out of the closet. Memories that highlight the undeniable fact that Emma has always been the golden child and I the disappointing second roll of the dice.

As a kid it didn't bother me too much—Emma adored and coddled me enough to make up for two disinterested mothers—but after she went to college things got ugly. So ugly I've never told my sister about all of it. If Emma knew, it might affect her relationship with Mom, and as much as I resent Renee sometimes, I don't want to do that to her. Or to Emma.

So I keep my mouth shut and let them have their

relatively happy and stress-free bond. Ruining it won't make my relationship with my mother any better. Only time travel and a personality transplant would have any hope of that, and Renee isn't a good candidate for either.

"And I would use the time travel for myself," I mutter as I pull onto the 101 headed north. "To go back and tell Jordan there's no way he's getting near me with a camera while I'm naked."

Though, if Jordan hadn't shot those photos, I never would have ended up camping out in Sonoma County long enough to hook up with the best fuck buddy in the entire world, or to learn that orgasms aren't as elusive as my previous lovers led me to believe. As painful and embarrassing as this situation has been, I wouldn't go back and change a thing—I'm *that* hooked on Rafe's body and the things he makes me feel.

It's an unnerving realization, but I shut down the trickle of foreboding before it can become more than a drip. Rafe and I are having an amazing time together, but we're both grown-ups and decent human beings. When it's time for this to end, we'll find a way to make "goodbye" as easy as falling into bed was in the first place.

Everything with Rafe is easy. It's one of the reasons he's so much fun to spend time with—no drama, no angst, no stress or mess or worrying that I'm going to say or do the wrong thing. I can just be completely myself in the company of a man who is completely himself, and it's all good. So good it seems like I'm always counting the minutes until I can see him again.

I arrive at A Better Way Shelter as the sun completes its slide toward the horizon, kissing the brown summer hills of the Dry Creek valley. Almost immediately, the air begins to cool, taking the edge off the July heat, a fact I greatly appreciate as I tag along with Tristan and Zoey to feed the horses.

"Wow, they look so much better than the last time I was here." I reach out to stroke the nose of a kind-eyed bay who trots eagerly to the fence. This crew of ten mares came from a farm where they'd been half starved to death before a neighbor called to report animal cruelty, but in just over a week their ribs are already less visible.

"They're doing so well," Zoey agrees, handing me a handful of baby carrots to disperse among the animals while Tristan fills the feed bins. "We're hoping to start taking applications for adoptions in a few months."

"But they're not saddle broken," Tristan says, a warning in his tone. "So that's going to slow the process down. A lot. We need to make sure we've got money on hand to keep them as long as a year if we need to."

"Under control." I pull out my flier designs for our Yappy Hour event and hand them over to Zoey. "I just need you guys to pick a design, and I'll get them printed and hung all over the county. Emma's going to hand them out to the winery owners at one of her networking events, and I've got a team of teen volunteers who are going to plaster Santa Rosa and surrounding cities while I continue my phone call campaign to reach out to top donors I've culled from your list."

"Thanks, Carrie." Tristan joins Zoey and me by the fence as the horses finish the last of the carrots in my outstretched palm and move on to the now full feeding troughs. "You're a lifesaver."

"My pleasure.," I say, lifting a hand to shade my face from the setting sun as I glance up into Tristan's face.

He looks so much like Rafe—same dark eyes and bronze god skin—but so different, too. Not any less handsome, but definitely more haunted, as if he's taking life twice as seriously to make up for his brother's devil-may-care attitude. The shadows under his eyes look even worse than the last time I stopped by, making me think Tristan could use some TLC as much as the horses he's helping bring back from the brink.

"This one," Zoey says, pulling my attention her way. She holds up the flier featuring bulldog puppies in martini glasses. "I love it. It's so insanely cute I can hardly stand it. But see what you think, boss."

Tristan shakes his head, refusing the papers Zoey holds out toward him. "I trust you. You've got a better grip on cuteness than I do. If you say that's the one, then that's the one."

Zoey grins. "All right. I'll go print them up."

"I can do that," I say, patting my purse. "I've got a zip drive with the file on it. I can just swing by the printer in town on my way home."

"No need," Zoey says. "We've got a great printer here. If you want to give me the drive, I can have them done in a few minutes. Cut out the middleman and spare you a trip."

I'm in no rush to hurry home—Rafe has to do inventory and place a parts order tonight and won't be available for playtime until later—but I hand over the zip drive anyway and thank Zoey. She promises to be right back with copies and beers for all and hurries into the main building, while Tristan and I wander over to the picnic tables with a view of the hills.

"Gorgeous." I take a deep breath, pulling in the scent of eucalyptus trees, fennel, and the sweet, salty smell of the hay baled nearby.

"The country life starting to grow on you, city girl?" Tristan asks, sitting on top of the picnic table with his boots on the wooden seat.

"It is." I cross my arms, amazed again at how fast the air goes from boiling hot to just-a-tad-chilly around here. "But I've always loved nature. It's the people in small towns who make me want to make a run for the nearest metropolis."

"I get it." Tristan squints out at the view, where the sunset glow makes the vineyards look like something out of a Renaissance painting. "There's not much anonymity in a small town. Everyone knows everyone else's business."

I sigh. "Yeah, but everyone knows my business these days. It's made the small-town thing less stressful."

"Sorry about that," he says. "I hate that you're going through this. I hate that so many men don't know how to behave themselves."

"It's fine. Or it's going to be fine. Scandals get forgotten pretty quickly in this day and age. There's always another salacious something on the horizon." I step onto the bench and sit beside him. "How about you? How are you holding up?"

Tristan lifts a tired shoulder and lets it fall. "Fine."

I hum beneath my breath. "Yeah, you look and sound fine."

His lips curve. "You people are going to give me a complex. Between you, Zoey, and the volunteers bringing me extra sandwiches, if I were the kind of person who stressed about my appearance, my confidence would be in the shitter."

"No way, dude, you're still totally smoking hot." I clap him encouragingly on the back, doing my best to reverse the damage I've unintentionally done.

I've been where he is, and the last thing you need when you're shacking up at the Heartbreak Hotel is well-meaning friends making you feel even worse than you do already.

"You just look sad is all I meant," I continue gently.

Tristan's chin dips closer to his chest as he lets out a soft laugh. "Yeah, well...I am. But it's okay. It's getting better."

"Are you sure? You don't have to pretend with me, you know. I'm a judgment-free zone about sadness and just about everything else."

He glances my way, his eyes steady and clear. "I'm sure. But thanks for caring."

"You're my brother-in-law's brother. And a wonderful person. Of course I care."

"I appreciate it." He smiles, his lips curving into an exact replica of Rafe's grin but without any of the trouble in it, leaving me tingle-free and proving I probably deserve the disaster that's plagued my love life.

Why do the troublemakers and heartbreakers make me tingle?

Why not sweet, honest, thoughtful gentlemen like Tristan?

"So what makes the judgment list?" He nudges my elbow with his, clearly ready to change the subject. "You said you were judgment-free about *almost* everything."

"Oh, I don't know." I lean back, my hands braced on the table behind me. "People who listen to country music unironically, maybe? Though Emma's developing a taste for it, and I love her, so probably not." I furrow my brow, scrolling through my mental list of repulsive things. "People who make canned seafood?"

Tristan pulls a face. "Canned seafood is an abomination."

"I know, right? I'm not a cat, don't try to feed me tuna you've ruined with gross processing and shoved into a can."

He shudders. "Or lobster you've mixed with corn and expect me to nurse back to life with milk."

"Canned chowder is repulsive. Do not want." I stick out my tongue with a gagging sound that makes Tristan laugh. "Yeah, I judge those people. Hard."

"Me, too." He glances over his shoulder. "But don't tell Zoey. She brings a tuna salad sandwich to work for lunch at least once a week."

I wave a hand through the cool air. "Oh no, we're not judging Zoey, just the people responsible for putting the seafood into the can in the first place. She's as much a victim of this sick conspiracy as anyone else."

"Agreed." His smile widens as he gently knocks his knee into mine. "Thanks for the talk. It cheered me up."

"Anytime." I pull him into a one-armed hug. "Next time we can discuss the abomination that is vanilla ice cream."

Tristan returns the embrace. "Vanilla ice cream does need to level up."

I nod. "Totally. Like, get a job, vanilla ice cream. I hate you."

"Hate who?" a deep voice asks from not far behind us.

I pull away from Tristan to see Rafe walking up the hill beside Zoey, holding two lightly sweating beers in one hand and looking good enough to pound in one big, long gulp. Seems like someone finished his work early, and someone else's night just got a whole lot sexier.

CHAPTER 16

RAFE

*I*t was just a friendly hug.

I *know* that. I know it the way I know that the sun is hot and ice-cold beer is a gift from the gods and that no matter how many pairs of matching socks I buy, I will always end up with a useless orphan hanging out in my drawer clogging up the joint. But that doesn't mean I enjoyed seeing Carrie in my brother's arms.

I didn't.

Not one fucking bit.

I enjoyed it so little that, after we finish our beers and Carrie agrees to leave her car at the shelter so she can join me for a night ride, my jaw remains clenched the entire trip out to the coast.

And when we get to my usual picnic spot, I don't say a word as I gather blankets from the saddlebags and an armful of wood from my hiding spot behind two rocks.

"You okay?" Carrie asks, trailing after me as I lead the way down the rock path to the secret ledge overlooking the churning ocean. It can be a tricky walk when it's cloudy, but tonight the moon shines over the midnight-blue waves below and casts the cliffs in a soft, pearl glow.

It would be beautiful if I weren't so *fucking* pissed for no *fucking* reason.

Even if Carrie and my brother *had* been hugging as more than friends—even if they were ripping each other's clothes off as often as they got the chance—I would have no right to feel jealous. Carrie and I are buddies with benefits, nothing more.

I don't want more. I truly don't.

So why are my panties in a fucking twist?

"Rafe?" Carrie's voice is gentle, but probing, making it clear she realizes something's wrong and that she isn't going to let it go.

But I'm not having that conversation. No way in hell am I telling her that seeing her arms around my brother made me want to throw her over my shoulder, hop on my bike, and keep driving until we're in another time zone.

"I'm fine. You?" I drop the firewood into the ring of stones and spread the thickest gray blanket out beside it. "Cold?"

"Not too cold. We don't have to build a fire if you don't want to."

"We'll build a fire." I toss the extra blankets onto the ground before turning back to Carrie. "But I need to do something else first."

Her lips part, but before she can respond, I've pulled her against me. My lips find hers in a bruising kiss, claiming her mouth with deep strokes of my tongue as I jerk her jacket over her shoulders and down her arms, summoning a moan from low in her throat as she rips her hands free and reaches for the close of my jeans.

Yes, this is what we need, a visceral reminder that we're about sex and pleasure, pure and simple, with no room for anything else.

We tumble to the blanket, tearing at each other's clothes while devouring each other like starving people. I pinch her nipples tight, rolling them between my fingers and thumb as I rub a rough hand between her legs, grinding the heel of my palm against her clit through her panties.

I don't have the patience for gentle or slow right now. I need to be inside her, fucking her hard, taking the only thing she's given me permission to demand.

As soon as her panties are off, I nudge her thighs wide and drive inside her pussy to the hilt, summoning a cry from her lips that I swallow with another penetrating kiss. I fuck her mouth with my tongue as I ride her, ramming into her slick heat, claiming her with sharp, brutal strokes as her nails dig into my shoulders and her breath comes in shallow gasps and sexy little whimpers.

For once, we don't talk. We fuck.

Or, more accurately, *I* fuck *her*. I *take* her, and in the process, I somehow manage to confess everything I've been trying to hide.

Not a single word is exchanged, but how much I want to possess her is clear in every kiss, every caress, every thrust deep into her body. I lay claim to her with my tongue, my fingers, my cock, making demands I have no right to make. But that doesn't stop me.

I can't stop. I can't pull back, I can't hide the crazy things she makes me feel.

I ride her until she comes screaming my name and when my balls start to clench, I make sure I'm buried as deep as possible in her pussy before I let go, coming with a force that wrenches animal sounds from deep in my chest as I mark her with my release.

For a long beat after, the only sounds are our labored breath, the thud of my pulse heavy in my ears, and the crash of the waves far below.

I don't know what to say. Or to think.

Finally, Carrie says in a soft voice, "I'm cold now, how about you?"

"On it." Feeling more awkward post-fuck than I have in years, I pull out, get dressed, and set about building the fire while Carrie pulls on her clothes behind me. My hands move on slow, methodical auto-pilot—arranging kindling and tinder beneath the larger chunks of wood and striking the matches—but inside my thoughts are racing.

What the fuck was that all about? What is wrong with me? And how the hell am I going to explain myself to Carrie when I have no clue why I'm losing my shit?

As the fire catches and spreads, Carrie pulls one of the blankets around her shoulders, staring into the flames that cast her somber face in a warm light. I shrug my sweater on and sit down beside her, wishing I could turn back time and redo the last twenty minutes. Yes, the sex was lava hot, but it wasn't honest or easy.

It was…complicated.

And now the energy between us is fraught. Carrie wasn't thrilled about being asked on a no-strings sex-cation, I can only imagine how spooked she's going to be once she fully processes the possessive energy I was channeling a few minutes ago.

"Want to head home, then?" I ask, though the words make my chest ache. I don't want to take her home. I want to take her in my arms, pull her close, kiss her forehead and tell her I'm sorry for being a dick.

"Why don't you do relationships?" She draws the blanket tighter around her shoulders as the wind picks up. "Did you just emerge from the womb that way?"

I hold my hands out to the fire as an excuse not to look at her.

So we're having this conversation, are we?

Fuck…

But I guess I shouldn't be surprised, and I owe her a truthful answer after the way I just behaved. "No," I say after a long beat. "I was about five when I realized long-term commitment wasn't for me."

"Bad kindergarten breakup?"

My lips curve. "That's when Dylan came to live with us. When my mom left."

"Left?" Carrie's brows lift. "Your dad?"

"And us," I say, ribs tightening. "She was so pissed about my dad's secret kid that she flew to Italy to hook up with this guy she used to date before she came to the States to go to college. Tristan and I didn't see her for six months. Tris was only two, so he doesn't remember, but…" I shrug, uncomfortable, but not as tied in knots as I usually am when talking personal shit. "It doesn't seem like that long now, but at five, six months felt like forever. An eternity. I didn't think she was ever coming back, and when she did..." I curl my hands into fists, watching the firelight flicker on my knuckles. "I wished she'd stayed away."

Carrie nods, studying me solemnly. "You were angry. You had every right to be."

I stretch my head to one side, but the knot in my neck only gets worse. "I guess so. But at the time she was just a reminder that my family was broken, and I didn't want to remember. I wanted to turn back time and have things be the way they use to be, or go forward the way we were, just me, my dad, and my brothers. It wasn't as warm or fun, but it was safe. Easy."

"I get that, too. Change is hard for kids. We're all creatures of routine. We need it to feel safe, especially as children."

I shrug. "For a long time, whenever she'd come to pick us up, I'd hide out in the woods and make Tristan go visit her alone. I hated how out of control I felt when I saw her. Like I could run forever but I'd never be free because the thing I was running from was trapped inside me."

Carrie shifts her foot until her boot rests gently on top of mine. She doesn't say a word, and there are layers of fabric and leather between us, but the touch helps. It takes the edge off the ugly memories.

She really is a good listener.

I squeeze her calf through the blanket in silent thanks. "We've got a good relationship now, but some things never changed. I love my mother and I forgave her a long time ago, but I never saw a reason to alter my thinking on relationships. Like you said, marriage isn't natural, and it certainly doesn't seem to work out that often."

Silence falls, and I figure that's the end of the conversation, until Carrie says, "It's crazy, isn't it? How much parents can mess you up. None of the men I dated had a chance to break me. I was already screwed-up way before I was old enough to date."

I squeeze her calf again, this time letting the touch linger. "I'm actually okay with my history. I wouldn't undo my mom leaving. Is that crazy?"

She looks up at me, her gaze clear, unguarded. "Why? Because the disillusionment would have come eventually? Better to get it over?"

My lips hook on one side. "That's about the size of it."

"I get it." Her hand emerges from her blanket cocoon to rest on my cheek, her thumb brushing lightly across my bottom lip. "But five is so young. If I could go back in time and talk some sense into your mother, I would. And I'd give baby Rafe a big hug. I bet he needed one."

My jaw clenches and emotion floods my chest, but I don't want to pull back or run from it. I want to lean in, to get close. I want to cut myself on the sharp edges of her compassion, to catch fire and burn in the light in her eyes. Even more dangerously, I want to kiss her, pull her body on top of mine, and show her how close I can get to really connecting.

Talk is cheap for me—always has been. It's something I can control and shape to meet my needs.

But touch…

Well, I proved again tonight that touch is where my edges blur. Where—if I'm not careful—fucking can become something so much more. Where a kiss can become "I want you" and skin hot against skin can become "I need you" and sliding inside a woman becomes an even bigger confession.

My lips have never formed the words, but my body has said "I love you" dozens of times. With Beverly, the girl who took my virginity in our hayloft when I was thirteen and she was fourteen and my boy-man brain was still too young to tell the difference between pleasure and love. With Nora—sweet, damaged Nora who drowned her pain in my body for a year before checking into an addiction treatment facility and never coming back to me the way she'd promised.

There were times with Vicky and Layla, too, and with Wendy, the leader of an all-girl biker gang with the biggest smile in the world, but nothing recently.

Nothing since my thirtieth birthday. Looking back, I know it was around then that something shifted inside of me. The protective shell around my heart expanded to take up more real estate, to encapsulate my entire self, ensuring no one gets too close, not even when we're naked.

Especially then.

The shield has a mind of its own. It knows when to firm up its boundaries, when to hold strong against pleasurable sensory input that could so easily be mistaken for something more. The shield protects the brain and the body from themselves. The shield is a friend, a weapon, a superpower.

The shield allows me to walk among the other mortal, suffering, needing, lost, and drowning people and keep myself above the fray. Without it, I'm as vulnerable as any other man, wandering around with my heart beating outside my chest and all the fears and desires I think I'm keeping so close exposed for the world to see.

I can take one look at either of my brothers and know exactly what they're feeling, what they're thinking, what they're afraid of losing or finding on any given day. And though I would die for either of them, I don't want to be like them.

I *can't* be like them. I've come too far to regress, to go back to being naked and shivering in the cold. I know how good it feels to be warm. To not only be clothed, but to be tricked out in impenetrable armor, riding atop a horse big enough to give me a clear view over the sea of humanity, where I can keep my eye on the prize.

There are things I want from life, things I'm willing to take risks for, but this isn't one of them. Love with another damaged person—someone who would make me feel less alone for a few months, a few years at best, before our sharp edges wear away the ties that bind, leaving us even more broken than we were before.

So I don't lean in. I don't kiss Carrie, even though every cell in my body is dying for a taste of her, howling for me to get her out of that blanket and under me, to push inside her and make her come for me, with me, crying out my name because I do things to her no other man has ever done.

I'm not special to Carrie, and she isn't special to me, and this has gone on long enough. I have to step back, to put enough distance between us that time and space can rush in and cool the heat, banish the longing, make me forget that I was ever this close to the edge, staring down into her big blue eyes and wondering if drowning in her might be worth losing all my hard-won control.

"It's late. I should take you home," I say. "Or back to your car. Whichever."

"Not to your place?" she asks, a challenge in her voice that I answer with a shake of my head.

"Not tonight."

She sighs but doesn't look away. "All right. My car. Better for me to drive home. Fewer questions in the morning about how I got there without the Mini Monster."

"You need a new car." I focus on putting out the fire while she gathers the blankets. "I've got a few recommendations I can send your way, things you could get for a couple grand after you trade in the monster."

"Thanks, I would appreciate that," she says.

"No problem." After the last of the smoke has died down, I lead the way back up the cliff trail, lighting the path with my phone until our eyes grow accustomed to the moonlight again, grateful for the wind and the fact that having a meaningful conversation on a motorcycle is damned near impossible.

We barely say three words on the way back to the

shelter—all the lights off, now, save the lamp in the parking lot and an orange glow from Zoey's apartment window—and after Carrie slides off next to her car, I don't turn off the bike.

"I should run," I say. "Still have some work to do before I hit the sack."

She hands her helmet over. "Sure. Good luck."

"Thanks. You, too." I say with a smile. "Drive safe."

She lifts a hand, holding it still in the air as I turn my bike around and head back onto the rural highway leading to the interstate. It's clear in the way she's standing, in the way she watches me leave, in the way her arm falls to her side, that she knows this isn't "goodbye for now." This is "the end."

With any other girl, that would be enough to give me the mental space I need, but not with Carrie. As long as she's sleeping in a bed less than fifteen minutes from mine, I'm going to keep thinking crazy thoughts.

I need more than mental space. I need physical distance.

As soon as I get home, I text Cal, owner of the Cadillac and my old partner. He's in his sixties now, but he taught me everything I know about Harley repair. He's more than capable of covering for me at the shop, and he's usually psyched to have an excuse to get out of the house. Cal, like most of my older friends, has a wife he barely speaks to anymore, with whom he has nothing in common except the two girls they raised and the four grandchildren they both adore.

Another reason not to take a step down the relationship road—I want a hell of a lot more from life than living with a stranger in exchange for kids and grand-kids. I'll love my brothers' babies, be the best uncle any rug rat could ever want, and never have to make those sad, stereotypical compromises.

As predicted, Cal is thrilled to fill in at the shop. He agrees to meet me bright and early tomorrow to get the keys and other instructions. As soon as we hang up, I start packing. It's been a while since I rode the coast highway, stopping to camp along the way. The time, stunning views, and hours spent alone in quiet contem-plation will be good for me.

In a few days—a week at most—I'll be back inside my armor, atop my horse, far from the emotional fray. I'll be able to see this thing with Carrie as a mistake safely avoided and maybe, eventually, as a fond memory of a sexy summer fling.

Soon, I'll be myself again, and I'll forget how close I came to falling in love, so close I can still taste Carrie's kiss lingering on my lips as I slip into a fitful sleep.

CHAPTER 17

CARRIE

To: Rafe_Hunter_Bikes
From: C.J.Haverford_Author
Subject: Every beat of my heart…

Dear Valentine,

It's been nearly a week since you dropped me off at my car and left town without saying a word. I can only assume that you're running away because I asked intrusive questions, you opened up to me, and now you're afraid that I want to move into your place, take my shoes off, and stay barefoot and pregnant for the next twenty years.

Well, you're right, Val…

I've fallen desperately in love with you, and all I can

think about is your big cock and your bigger heart and how desperately I want to spend every waking minute with both of you. I was half a person and you made me whole. I was a soggy puzzle piece and you dried me off and showed me where I fit in the bigger picture. I was lost in the wilderness, dying of dehydration, and your cock was the divining rod that led me to water.

If you don't come home soon, I will waste away to nothing and on my tombstone it will read "Caroline Haverford: Died of a Broken Heart and A Bereaved Pussy."

Are you still reading?

Are you freaking out or laughing?

Maybe sighing in relief?

I hope one of the latter. It's hard to communicate tone in an email, but I hope you know me well enough to realize I'm jerking your chain.

Yes, I would rather be jerking your cock, because fucking you was a lot of fun, but you don't have to worry about any of the rest of it, Rafe. I'm not in love with you. I'm not mourning you. I'm not sitting here waiting to pounce and cling to your leg until you see we're perfect together.

I don't want anything from you, except for you to know that I had a great time and I'm happy to part ways as friends the way we planned.

So, if you're staying away on my account, feel free to come home. Dylan doesn't seem worried—apparently you've got a habit of ghosting for long stretches of time? —but Tristan has been asking probing questions. I think he suspects something. I've denied everything, but the best way to put him off the scent would be for you to come home and for everyone to act normal.

And I'd love for you to come to the Yappy Hour event if you're back in time. It's going to be a lot of fun. Bring a date if you want. I don't mind at all. I'll probably try to rustle up someone to bring, myself, just so I'll have someone to dance with during the slow songs. I love dancing. How about you?

See, we can have normal conversations about normal things.

Everything will be fine.

Come home, or at least let someone know you're alive. I have no designs on your heart, but I would like to know your body is okay. You need your body to keep walking around in.

And it would be a shame for the world to lose a cock

like yours in its prime, before it's had the chance to pleasure more of the female population.

You really do have a gift, Valentine.

Thanks for sharing it with me for a little while.

Yours in friendship,
Carrie

CHAPTER 18

*A*t first, I think I'm still dreaming.

The email comes through when I'm at the height of the fever that's been plaguing me since I set up my tent on Pismo beach. But considering it's the first good dream I've had so far, I get a drink of water and take another look at my inbox.

Sure enough, it's still there, an email from Carrie. She's worried about me, she wants me to check in, and she wants me to keep her barefoot and pregnant for the next twenty years.

I squint at that line again, rereading until I understand that part was a joke.

And weirdly, in my feverish, sweating, aching, summer-flu-induced haze, the realization makes me sad.

I like the thought of knocking her up. I like the thought of her barefoot in my kitchen with me, drinking coffee and cracking jokes and reading the

LILI VALENTE

morning paper. I like the thought of her missing my body, and I can't stop imagining all the things I want to do to hers as soon as I'm not sick or burning up with fever or constantly dying of thirst.

Right then, I decide I'm going home.

Time and space aren't working this time. She's all I can think about, dream about, fantasize about as I crawl to the front flap of my tent and stare out at the churning ocean. I want her here with me, watching the sunset and munching on saltine crackers. Better yet, I want to be back home with her, alone in our blanket fort, hidden away in a cocoon of warmth and pleasure.

"Cool and pleasure," I mumble, taking another swig of water. I'm still hot, flushed, and not nearly one hundred percent, but I'm getting better. By tomorrow, the day after at the latest, I'll be well enough to ride home.

And then I'll tell Carrie in person what I think about being just friends.

That it's stupid. And that I'm stupid. And that we would both be stupid to let something this good slip through our fingers without at least giving ourselves a shot to get the relationship thing right.

Hopefully, she'll hear me out with an open mind. Reading between the lines, I can't help but think she cares more than she's letting on.

I open the email and read it again. And again. And again, until I fall asleep with the phone cradled against my chest and visions of Carrie dancing in my head.

CHAPTER 19

My niece is an angel from heaven who I am privileged to have in my life. I would give her a kidney. I would throw myself in front of a bus or a pack of rabid wolves or a stampede of zombie buffalo for this child. I would take a bullet for this princess who breaks my heart with her smile and heals it up again with her slobbery baby kisses.

But sometimes she's a real pain in the ass.

Huge.

Enormous.

So large that if she were actually a boil on my backside, I wouldn't be able to get off this bench to run after her because I would be weighed down by the size of the junk on my trunk.

Thankfully, however, her pain-in-ass-ness if figurative, and I'm able to bolt from my seat, sprint across the wood chips at the toddler playground in the town square, and grab Mercy before she puts a handful of someone else's melted ice cream cone—currently oozing all over the merry-go-round—into her mouth.

"No, Mercy," I say for the fifteen thousandth time since my niece spotted the fallen cone, grabbing her pudgy wrist in the nick of time and holding her sticky fingers away from her mouth. "That's dirty. Yuck."

"No!" Mercy bellows back, making use of her newest vocabulary word.

"It's not yours, buddy," I continue in my calmest tone as I guide her toward the bathrooms. "That's someone else's, and it's dirty."

"No! No! No!" Mercy wails into my face, the fearsome gleam in her eyes making me laugh even as the moms on the closest bench shoot concerned glances our way.

"You look like you want to take my head off," I mutter beneath my breath, clinging tight to my niece's arms as she tries to pull away. "Come on, Mercy. We need to wash hands."

"No! Noooooooo!" Mercy's spine arches, and a moment later she goes boneless, melting into a puddle at my feet, facedown in the wood chips.

"Stop it, Mercy, you're going to scratch your cheeks."

"Nooooo!" She thrashes like a fish ripped from the cool depths of her rivery home, all outrage and muscle. "No! No! No!"

"Geez, give me a break, kid." I readjust my grip on her squirming babyness while breaking out in a sweat beneath my shirt.

I would have called it a chilly evening a few minutes ago. But that was before Mercy decided to teach me a lesson in what it takes to win a war of wills with the most stubborn toddler ever born.

Of course, this would never have happened if Rafe hadn't run off. If he'd stayed, I would be out with him right now, getting busy in a waterfall or at a delightfully creepy drive-in or down by the ocean while the waves make the cliffs vibrate the way he makes my body vibrate, setting me to humming at the perfect frequency.

Instead, I breached his emotional firewall, he ran, and I was therefore on hand to offer to babysit while Emma chairs her wine road event meeting.

Now I'm going to come home with a wood-chip-scratched and splintered-up baby with filthy ice-cream hands, and Emma will never trust me to care for her daughter again.

And why should she?

I'm a wreck. A mess. A formerly together person who is watching my house of cards tumble down around me, marveling that I ever thought I had built something solid.

The softening book sales and lingering ill-will generated by the leaked pictures are symptoms of a deeper problem. *I'm* the real disease. *I'm* the fool who thought it would be okay to quit my perfectly decent job managing a well-respected toy store to write full time. *I'm* the one who spent my first few years of royalty checks on a down payment for a condo in a nice part of Berkeley, naively assuming the checks would keep flowing in.

But there are no guarantees in life, especially a life

spent playing pretend for a living. I should have known that. I should have been more careful. I should have kept my steady job and continued to write in my spare time—who cares if that meant I had to write more slowly?

And it's not just my work life that's fucked to hell. I should have kept my family at arm's length and my mother at least a state and a half away. If I had, Mom and I wouldn't be sniping at each other like I'm sixteen again, and Emma wouldn't have to learn that I'm shitty with kids and should never be trusted with her loin fruit.

Most importantly, I should have kept my dating life casual. I should have kept things with Rafe fuck-buddy easy, instead of reaching out to probe the soft, vulnerable places beneath his tough guy exterior. Yes, he's the most fascinating, sexy, confident, magnetic man I've met in years—maybe *ever*—and yes, the chinks in his armor make him even more irresistible, but that's no excuse for playing with fire.

I should be glad he's gone.

Grateful that he saved me from myself.

Instead, as I wrestle Mercy from the ground, getting kicked hard in the stomach as thanks for my efforts to keep her germ-free, all I can think about is how much she reminds me of him. No matter how much I would like for her to be a more passive and agreeable child at this precise moment, I love this part of her.

I love her spit and fire. I love her fierce will and her passion for exploration and her determination to discover every inch of a world that ignites her curiosity.

And maybe I was starting to love that about Rafe, too, just a little.

Maybe more than a little. Maybe enough that writing that email a couple days back was a hell of a lot harder than I expected it to be. Maybe enough that I should pack up and get out of here before he comes back...

"I should," I tell Mercy when we're finally inside the remarkably clean park bathroom and I've got her hands soaped up and under the warm water. "I should go home before it's too late. Hiding isn't solving anything, anyway. I'm worse off than when I came here to get away from it all."

Mercy looks up at me, blue eyes wide and curious. "Ba?"

I sigh. "No, I didn't bring the ball. I'm a loser. I'm sorry."

Mercy giggles. "Ba!"

I shake my head. "No ball."

The baby laughs again, thrusting her hands into the air, sending water droplets flying.

"Well, I'm glad someone's amused by my poor life choices." I grin as I hand her a paper towel and she jumps up and down with it, spinning in a circle with it held overhead like an umbrella, turning it into a toy because that's what kids do. They play when they should be taking care of business, and turn business into play.

Maybe that's my problem.

I never grew up. Not all the way. Not the way a

person is supposed to, where they gain maturity and realize that not everything in life is a toy.

People aren't toys.

Penises aren't toys.

"Well, that's not entirely true," I mutter to myself as I open the door to the bathroom and Mercy toddles outside ahead of me.

Penises are more like toys than a lot of other things. Penises are always up for a good time, don't take themselves too seriously, and enjoy being fondled more than your average bouncy ball or jar of Play-Doh. Penises are forgiving, too, willing to forget the time you left them at the playground, or made them attend a tea party with dolls they don't care for, as long as you'll take them out of the toy box again.

In a moment of synchronicity that sends a shiver across my skin, the proof of my theory is standing near the toddler-sized slide, grinning as he kneels down to offer outstretched arms to Mercy. The baby spots her uncle and makes a beeline for Rafe with a happy squeal that leaves no doubt we're both happy to see him.

"There's my girl." Rafe lifts Mercy high into the air, grinning up at her while she kicks her arms and legs in spontaneous celebration. "Are you having fun at the playground?"

"No!" Mercy yells, followed by a wicked giggle that makes Rafe and I both laugh.

He turns to me, tucking Mercy into the crook of one arm, his smile fading as his eyes meet mine. But it dims only a watt or two and, judging from his expression, he's not unhappy to see me. "Hey, there. Dylan said you two were down here causing trouble."

"Lies," I say solemnly, playing it cool as I try to read his expression. "Mercy was the one trying to eat ice cream off the merry-go-round. I was nobly defending her from germs and stickiness. I'm practically a hero."

"No. No. No," Mercy says, mimicking my haughty tone so perfectly I can't help but reach for her ribs.

"Are you making fun of me, little squirrel?" I tickle her, fingers dancing as she bats me away with chubby arms, giggling. "What happened to respecting my authority? I told you to respect my authority!"

Mercy laughs harder, until her cheeks flush bright red and Rafe is forced to set her on her feet before she squirms free and falls to the ground.

"Get back here, you!" I pretend to chase after her, fingers clawed, but I give her plenty of time to escape to the safety of her favorite red tunnel. She crawls away, giggling and babbling to herself, while I stand, breath rushing out as I glance back at her delicious uncle.

"So, what's up?" I ask, fighting to keep my tone casual. In a pair of faded black jeans and a threadbare green flannel, he shouldn't be so beautiful that he makes my pulse race and my lungs struggle to pull in a deeper breath. But he is. Even more handsome than he was in the glow of the firelight that night on the coast.

I'd assumed our friends-with-benefits status had been snuffed out along with that campfire, but now here he is, running a hand through his shaggy hair and studying me with eyes that look more hopeful than fearful.

But hopeful for what?

Until I have a better idea, my cards are staying glued to my chest. Keeping my expression as neutral as possible, I turn to check on Mercy, knowing better than to take my eyes off of her for more than a second or two. The girl is a disaster magnet and will put literally anything into her mouth—flowers, rocks, garbage, an old shoe, spiders that are crawling across the carpet, you name it.

"I got your email." Rafe shifts to stand behind me, making me powerfully aware of his body heat and how much I want to lean back against him and draw his arms around me. The urge to touch him is so powerful I don't know how well I'm going to be able to pull off the "just friends" thing. At least in the near future.

"Yeah?" I peek up at him before glancing back to the playground, where Mercy is very involved in shouting something unintelligible into the plastic speaker near the tic-tac-toe rollers.

"Yeah. At first, I thought I'd dreamt it," he says. "I had a fever for a few days while I was camped on the beach near Pismo. Made it hard to tell what was real and what was wishful thinking."

"Bummer. That's not a fun way to spend a vacation," I say, even as my brain nibbles at the phrase "wishful thinking."

So, does that mean he was hoping I would give him the all-clear, no-worries signal? That he's relieved we'll never devour each other like a last meal ever again?

The hope butterfly wafting cautiously through my chest shivers, as if sensing impending frost.

"No, it wasn't fun." He steps off the concrete ledge down into the wood chips, bringing our faces closer to level, making it impossible to keep from staring into his warm eyes. "But it was enlightening. While I was tossing and turning and sweating in my tent, I kept dreaming about you."

My brows lift. "Yeah?"

He nods slowly, holding my gaze with an intensity that makes my heart beat faster. "You were walking by my bed, carrying trays full of drinks. I wanted one of the glasses of water sweating on your tray more than anything in the world. I was dying for it, dying for you to hold it to my mouth so I could suck down every drop, but you never stopped to offer. You didn't even turn to look at me."

"I'm sorry." My lips turn down at the edges as I huff in laughter. "Dream me sounds like a jerk."

"She wasn't a jerk." He shoves his hands into his jeans pockets, glancing down at the ground before peering up at me through locks of that thick, sexy hair I love to wind around my fingers while he's kissing me. "I was the jerk. I was lying there waiting for someone to give me something I hadn't even had the balls to ask for. What kind of entitled piece of shit does that?"

My laugh is anxious this time. I cast a glance around the small park, checking on Mercy—still yelling into the speaker—while I make sure no one is close enough to hear us. "Language, Hunter. There are small folk about."

"Shit," he mutters, color creeping into his cheeks, which is pretty damned adorable. "Shoot, I mean. Sorry. I haven't done this in a long time. Ever, really. I'm pretty fu—" He bites off the word with a shake of his head. "Pretty nervous."

"Why are you nervous?" The hope butterfly flutters its wings faster. "Because you want to ask me for a glass of water?"

He steps closer. "The glass of water was symbolic."

"I figured," I murmur, lips curving.

"Yeah, so... I think I was wrong about relationships."

I blink, my heart lurching. "Yeah?"

He nods. "Yeah. What about you? Think there might be room in your life for something more than a fling? Assuming the guy was a great piece of ass, committed to making you laugh, and generally a decent person who swears he won't ever treat you badly or tell anyone that you snore when you're really tired?"

My smile crashes across my face. "I don't snore. But...yeah, I could be open to that."

"So, you want to go on a date?" he asks softly, his lips curving until his grin is as wide as mine. "A real date, no hiding. And another date after that. And maybe we just...see where things go from there, while also *not* seeing other people."

I laugh. "You mean date exclusively?"

"Yeah, that's what I meant." His shoulders relax away from his ears as his hands come to rest on my hips, sending a rush of heat and relief through me. "I don't know if I'll be very good at this at first. But I want to be. Think you can put up with me until I figure out how to be a decent boyfriend?"

"Aw, an official boyfriend," I tease, my arms going

around his neck. "I haven't had one of those in a long time. Not since college, in fact."

His brow furrows. "Is that not what people call it anymore? Am I old and lame?"

"No. You're not old or lame. You're young and awesome and I definitely want you to be my sexy boyfriend. Though, I think we should keep it on the down low as far as the family is concerned. Just for a little while."

"Before we have the talk, make sure I'm not going to screw things up?"

"No. Make sure it's really what we both want. I don't have the greatest track record, either, you know," I confess. "And I'm causing my family enough stress right now. Jordan sicced his lawyer on me yesterday. He's claiming he helped me plot the book I'm writing now and deserves half the royalties."

Rafe's expression goes stormy. "What the hell is up with this guy?"

"I don't know," I say with a sigh. "Maybe he's crazy. Maybe he's just vindictive. I don't know anymore, I just want it all to go away. But at this point, it looks like we're headed to court, one way or another."

Rafe's lips part, but before he can speak, a sharp, high-pitched wail sounds from the playground, followed by a familiar howl. Rafe and I break apart, turning to see Mercy at the base of the slide, tears streaming down her cheeks. I break into a run with Rafe close behind, and scoop Mercy up seconds before the next toddler emerges from the slide tunnel.

"What happened Mercy?" I ask, smoothing her blond

curls from her forehead as I scan her face. "Did you get an owie?"

"Owie," she echoes in a pitiful wail, holding up her hand. Her palm is red and there are scratch marks, but she didn't break the skin. I'm guessing her distress is more about the shock of discomfort rather than the intensity of the pain, which means there's only one medicine that will do.

"Oh, poor baby." I take her hand, bringing it to my lips. "There. Three kisses. Mwuah, mwuah, mwuah. Does that feel better? You need more?"

She nods as she shifts in my arms, holding her boo-boo out to Rafe, who immediately bends low, pressing a soft kiss to the baby's hand and making my ovaries explode. The last thing on my mind right now is making babies, and wondering what kind of dad Rafe would be has been so far off my radar that the words "Rafe" and "Father" might as well exist in different hemispheres.

But now, watching him kiss his niece's tiny fingers while murmuring sweetly to her that he's sorry she got hurt, I'm struck by the certainty that this man would be an incredible dad. The kind of dad who would never let you down or make you feel like you were a pain in his ass he wished wasn't hanging around his neck demanding time, money, and attention for eighteen years. Rafe would love his children the way he loves the little girl diving into his arms for "scratchy kisses."

I watch Rafe brush his stubbly cheek gently against Mercy's before he kisses the plump, pink skin, making her giggle, and a tidal wave of emotion swells inside me.

I could fall in love with this man, I realize, the truth crystallizing in the cool evening air. I could fall in love with him and want a life and a future and babies with him.

His eyes suddenly cut my way, his gaze capturing mine before I can rearrange the sappy expression on my face.

But thankfully, I'm saved by a mom with a Band-Aid.

"Does she need one of these?" the brunette from the bench asks, holding out a box of Dora the Explorer Band-Aids. "I always carry some in my diaper bag. Caley manages to get hurt at least twice a day."

"She doesn't really need one," I say with a smile. "But I'm sure she'd love to put one on, anyway, if you've got one to spare. Band-Aids are one of her favorite things."

Mercy agrees in a stream of baby babble, making the grown-ups laugh as I take a Band-Aid and affix it to her tiny hand. "Thanks so much," I tell Brunette Mom, who waves away my thanks.

"No worries," she says. "She looks exactly like you two, by the way. So cute. A perfect mix of Mommy and Daddy."

"Thanks." Rafe bounces Mercy in his arms as he winks at me.

"What?" he asks in a softer voice as Brunette moves away and we release Mercy back into the wild. "She *does* look like you. And she has the Hunter chin. And eyebrows. Lucky for her, since you and Emma are eyebrow deficient."

"I am not eyebrow deficient," I huff, propping my fists on my hips.

Rafe makes a judgmental face. "They're so blond you can hardly see them, Caroline. Seriously, you're lucky the rest of you is so smoking hot or those wimpy brows would be a deal breaker."

"Oh, they would, huh?" I shake my head as he pulls me into his arms, grinning down at me.

"I'm kidding. You're perfect. So perfect I want to have you for dessert after I take you to dinner. Seven okay? Pick you up by the Murphy bed place?"

"Seven is perfect," I say. "And I'll bring an overnight bag."

"That's the best news I've heard all day." The delight in his smile assures me that he means it. And the kiss he presses to my cheek is a mixture of sexy and sweet unlike anything I've felt in a long time.

It's terrifying. And exciting. And by the time he waves goodbye and I push Mercy's stroller back onto the sidewalk, the hope butterflies in my chest have multiplied.

It's a damned butterfly parade in there.

A festival.

And it feels completely, fucking amazing.

CHAPTER 20

RAFE

*G*etting older is more satisfying than I thought it would be. In my twenties, I dreaded thirty. It sounded so much closer to the grave than twenty-nine.

But at thirty-two, I realize that age has its benefits. When I was younger, I barreled through life, charging into each new adventure without stopping to soak up the experience. To pause, to observe, or to lock memories away for safekeeping.

At twenty-something I didn't have the sense to realize how precious memories are, let alone recognize a life-changing moment from a pedestrian one.

But now, as I savor the last bite of a shared crème brulée while the most beautiful woman I've met beams at me across the table, I do my best to wrap this memory up in protective paper. I want to remember the way the candlelight makes Carrie's eyes dance, the way she licks whipped cream from her fingertip, the way she watches me over the rim of her wine glass, hunger and happiness mixing in her expression.

Most of all, I want to remember this new softer, easier smile of hers. The one that means she trusts me enough to drop the drawbridge and to let me within shouting distance of her heart. I can't see it yet—let alone touch it or lay claim to it—but at least I've got a shot.

A chance.

An invitation…

"Want to come to a party with me next weekend?" I ask, taking her hand. "A friend of mine is opening a whiskey bar in Marin. We could drink too much whiskey, get a hotel room, see how much damage we can inflict on each other's bodies."

She grins, trouble sparking to life in her eyes. "Sounds good. As long as you go in with an understanding that whiskey makes me wild."

"As long as it makes your clothes come off at the same time, I'm game." I squeeze her cool fingers. "I like you wild."

"I've noticed." She leans closer, only to stop halfway to my lips as she curses and ducks her head, covering her face with her hand. "Oh God, no."

"What is it? What's wrong?"

"My mother is here," she hisses, curling closer to the table. "Across the room. By the bear holding the menus."

I glance casually over my shoulder, spying the older blonde at a table with an older man with long gray hair, who's channeling some serious Willie Nelson energy, but making it work. Renee is laughing brightly at something he's said, seeming oblivious to her daughter's presence.

"She didn't see you, did she?" I ask, turning back to Carrie.

"No, not yet, but she's a bloodhound. She'll sniff me out." She slides lower in her chair, until her chin is inches from her dessert plate. "We have to get out of here or there's no way anything's staying quiet. She'll give Emma an earful the second she gets to a phone. And she won't make it look good. She disapproves of every decision I've ever made, and banging my brother-in-law's brother is not going to be an exception to the rule."

I motion for the check. "Why?"

"Because we're complicated, obviously. For the rest of the family," she says, giving me a "what are you smoking" look. "You know that. We've talked about it."

"No, I mean why does she disapprove of all your decisions? Seems to me you've made some pretty good ones. You're a successful writer, beloved by children and girls I'm too dumb to realize are still children."

This gets a smile out of her, but only for a second. "I don't know."

"You don't?" I tug my wallet out of my jeans, dropping my credit card on the tray before the waitress can set it on the table. She thanks me and goes to run the card as I turn my attention back to Carrie. "You really don't know?"

"Well, sure...I guess I do," she says in a timid voice I barely recognize. "But I don't want to talk about it. Not right now."

I start to apologize, but our server has already returned with our check. As I sign, I nod toward the door. "Why don't you sneak out first? I'll follow at a respectable distance, meet you at the bike."

"Thanks." Carrie scoots out of her chair and is out the door so fast I have only a few seconds to admire how incredible she looks in just jeans and a purple-and-white striped T-shirt.

Frustrated with Renee for marring the memories Carrie and I were making tonight, I tuck my wallet back into my jeans and amble out into the cool summer evening. Monte Rio is closer to the river, and there's a chill in the air to prove it. When I reach my bike, I pull my emergency fleece from my saddlebag, intending to offer it to Carrie for the ride home. But when I turn to scan the parking lot outside the Big Bear Steakhouse, and the people milling around in front of the old movie theater across the street, she's nowhere to be seen.

Finally, I spot a flash of purple and blond down by the river, barely visible above the slope of the rocky beach.

I cross the street and head toward the water, finding Carrie sitting on a picnic table with her arms wrapped around her torso, watching the river roll by in the dim light from the porches of the shops and restaurants behind us.

"There you are." I climb up to sit beside her, holding out the fleece. "Thought you might want this."

"Thank you, that's thoughtful." She takes the fleece, pulling it on and rolling up the sleeves. It's enormous, but the soft gray material looks good on her. She looks cozy, snuggle-able, which goes to show how off book I am at this point. I lust after women, I don't crave a good, long snuggle session. But the fact remains that all I want to do right now is hold her.

So I do, pulling her close, throat going tight as she wraps her arms around me and rests her head on my chest.

"I'm sorry," I whisper. "I didn't mean to push or pry. For a guy who likes his privacy, I can be a nosey bastard sometimes."

"It's okay. Me, too. Being nosey is a good way to get people talking about themselves, leaving them less time and energy to talk about me."

I grunt. "We're a pair, huh?"

"We are." She lifts her head, looking up into my eyes. "But you were game that night by the beach, and I really liked learning more about your past. So..." She takes a deep breath and lets it out slow. "For a long time after my parents split up, my mom dated a bunch of jerks who treated her like shit."

"There are a lot of jerks out there."

Carrie's lips curve a little as she nods. "There are. And Renee fell in love with every one of them. Then she met Gary. He was a professor at a prestigious university, loved theater and live music like she did, and never made her pay for dinner or feel bad about our shitty little apartment. When Emma went to college, Mom and I moved into a smaller place so Renee could save up to help Emma pay for grad school. It was a dump, but Gary didn't look down on her for it. He helped her patch up the dents in the walls, paint the place, install some new cabinets, and in a few months, he had it looking downright swanky. He even hung fairy lights in my room for me so I could pretend I was going to sleep under the stars."

"Sounds good so far," I say cautiously. I can already tell this story isn't going to end well, however. I can feel it in the tension making her slim back feel like marble beneath my fingers.

"Yeah, he was pretty great." She sighs. "He also liked kids—had two of his own and wished he'd had more with his ex-wife, he said. I was fifteen, but I looked eleven or twelve. Thirteen on a good day, when I wore my shit-kicker boots and my eyeliner wasn't too smeared. Gary treated me like a much younger kid— bringing me candy and cartoon DVDs, shit like that— but I didn't mind. It was nice to have a father figure type person pay attention to me. I pretended to be this jaded badass at school and with my mom, but I missed my dad. It hurt that he was more interested in whatever crazy project he was working on at the moment than Emma or me."

"I get it," I say, squeezing her shoulder. "You know I do. It doesn't matter how old you are, it hurts when a parent leaves."

She nods, snuggling closer to my chest, making me feel even more protective. Making me hope like hell this story doesn't end the way I think it's headed. But I'm a realist, and I know a woman like Carrie isn't trying to disappear into my ribcage because she had a nice older friend who made her feel loved when she needed it.

"So I didn't discourage him when he tickled me or

teased me," she says softly. "I liked it when we'd watch movies on the couch, with my mom under one of his arms and me under the other. And the first time he hugged me and it went on a little too long, I thought I was imagining things."

My jaw locks, and the hand not smoothing up and down Carrie's back balls into a fist, but I don't say anything. I don't want to interrupt her or make it any harder for her to get to the end of this. Once you start a dark story, you have to get to the end. If you don't, you leave the story buried inside you, where no light can touch it or break its darkness into smaller pieces.

"But then he did it again. And again." She pauses, swallowing with an audible gulp. "Then he touched me through my clothes in places he shouldn't have touched me, and I knew the next time it happened he would take it farther. As soon as he left that day, I went to my mom and told her what was happening."

"Tell me she was there for you," I say softly. "Or I'm not sure Renee and I are going to be able to get along."

"She believed me right away," Carrie says, allowing some of the tension to seep from my shoulders. "She broke it off with him and took me to counseling. She would have taken it to the police, but I begged her not to. I was too embarrassed. I didn't want anyone to know that a guy old enough to be my dad had been the first person to feel me up."

I wrap both arms around her, hugging her tight, grateful when she returns the embrace, taking the comfort I so much want to give.

"But things were shitty between my mom and me

171

after that," she continues, pulling out of my arms and brushing her hair from her face. "She never said anything flat out, but it seemed like she resented me for taking away the only person who'd made her happy in so long. Back then, I thought she blamed me for what happened, like I'd asked for it by wearing skimpy pajamas around the house or something."

"You didn't ask for anything. You were a kid. He was a grown-up and a creep."

She nods, gaze fixed on the hands fisted in her lap. "I know that now. And I know my mom was probably just sad and mad, not sad or mad *at me*. But at the time I was just so angry and hurt." She lets out a soft laugh. "I made her life hell and gave new meaning to the rebellious teenager cliché. It's a miracle I made it out of high school alive. I did so much stupid stuff, and I know there were times when Renee wanted to strangle me with her bare hands."

I rest a hand on her knee. "You were a kid in pain. People in pain do stupid shit, but kids in pain are really dumb. They can't help it. They're not emotionally equipped to deal. I remember. It's why I cut my nephews more slack than Dylan does. Being a teenager is a fucking nightmare, even if everything is going mostly okay, let alone after something like what that man did to you."

"Thanks." Her lips curve before settling back into softness. "So that's the story of my mom and me. It gets better, it gets worse, but we've never been really close since then. At this point, I don't know that we ever will be. Especially not as long as I keep giving her things to disapprove of."

"Like dating me," I say, pushing on before she can confirm my hunch. "Well, too bad, Renee. I don't give a fuck what she thinks, and it's going to take a lot more than a disapproving parent to scare me away."

Carrie's grin finds its legs this time. "Yeah? Like what? Finding out I secretly hate motorcycles?"

I pause, brows lifting. "Do you hate motorcycles?"

She laughs. "No, I don't. I love riding with you. I just wanted to see what kind of face you'd make." Her grin is positively wicked. "It was as entertaining as I'd hoped."

I narrow my gaze. "I live to entertain, but no, learning you didn't like riding with me wouldn't scare me away. I'd probably just break down and buy the Cadillac. Cal's been tempting me with it for years, but I keep waiting for him to drop the price." I brush her hair from her face, tucking it behind her ear as the cool breeze does its best to blow it back again. "But for you, Trouble, I would pay a couple grand over Blue Book."

"Be still my heart." She presses a dramatic hand to her chest, but I can tell she's touched. Mocking tone or not, a part of her means it, and a part of me is already figuring out how soon I can buy that car. I want to see Carrie's face when I tell her it's mine and we can bang in the backseat whenever we like.

But for now, we need a bed, and I can't wait to get her to mine.

"Get out of here?" I ask.

"Yes, please," she says, slipping her hand into mine. "I

know we talked about catching a movie, but I'd really rather go get naked with you. If that's okay."

I nod solemnly. "It's very okay. The okay-est."

She grins. "I like you when you're all relaxed and sweet and letting me in."

"Yeah, well..." I shrug. "I'm pretty likable. Lick-able, too. All freshly showered and ready for your inspection."

Carrie's eyes narrow. "Did you put on the aftershave that tastes like honey and pine needles?"

"I did."

She squeezes my fingers as she stands, jumping off the bench. "Then let's go, psycho. I have licking to do."

We race each other up the riverside beach, and I let her win so I can watch her ass wiggle inside her jeans. And yes, I'm dying to get back home and get her clothes off, but I also relish every second of the ride home with her arms wrapped tight around me and her cheek resting on my shoulder. I love being close to her, in all different ways, and I just want to keep getting closer.

I'm falling so hard I don't think I could stop if I tried. Good thing I don't want to stop. I want to go and keep going until we see how far down this love road we can get.

CHAPTER 21

CARRIE

*A*ll the way home, all I can think of is kissing him. Not throwing him on his bed and ravaging him, not fucking like orgasm-starved savages until we're both boneless and spent.

Just...kissing.

His mouth on mine, his hands on my face, my fingers in his hair, our lips confessing with a touch all the things they're too afraid to speak out loud.

Things like...you're special. You're the person I didn't think I would ever find. You're my unicorn sighting, my portal at the back of the wardrobe. You are all the magical things I didn't believe existed, but better, because you're real.

And you're mine.

Or close to being mine. Closer than anyone has been in a long, long time.

After Rafe shuts off the engine, neither of us says a word. We simply melt into each other. We kiss up the stairs to his apartment and through the darkened living room to his bedroom door, where he sweeps me into his arms.

"I've never been carried to bed before," I whisper.

"What kind of losers have you been dating, woman?"

"The skinny, artistic kind who don't weigh much more than I do."

He smiles as he kisses me, making our teeth bump together through our lips. "Good. I like knowing I can kick your exes' asses if needed."

"Not needed," I say as he lays me down on his soft quilt, sending a shiver of anticipation dancing across my skin. "They're mostly friends now. Or glad to be rid of me. Or both."

"Idiots." Rafe slowly, deliberately lengthens himself on top of me, nudging my thighs apart so he can settle between them, making my nerve endings hum. "But their loss is my gain. Is it cheesy to admit that I'm pretty fucking excited about you being my girl?"

"No." I wrap my arms around his neck and my legs around his hips, chest going tight. "It's sweet, and I love it."

And I think I could love you. Maybe a part of me already does, I add silently because I know it's too soon.

Way too soon.

But it's true. This isn't infatuation or a rebound or a fling, and it doesn't matter that we've only been seeing each other a few weeks. I've dated men for months and never felt as close to them as I do to Rafe right now, with him holding my gaze as he rocks against me through our clothes, letting me feel how much he wants me.

My lips part in a gasp and his eyes darken, but neither of us looks away.

"I could come just from this," he says, grinding against me with long, languid thrusts. "That's how hot you get me, Caroline."

"Me, too." I lift my hips to meet his, a heavy ache spreading through my core. "I'm already so close."

"Don't come," he says in a commanding tone that makes my breath catch. "Not until I tell you to. Can you do that for me, Trouble?"

I arch a brow. "You want to be the boss tonight?"

"I want to steer," he says in a husky voice. "I want to know you trust me to take you to the edge. Do you trust me that much, baby?"

I nod, heart slamming against my ribs even as uneasiness flutters through my chest. "But what if I can't stop myself? Seriously, I'm so close I can taste how good it's going to feel."

"You're stronger than you give yourself credit for." He reaches for the hem of his shirt, pulling it over his head, revealing his sculpted chest with the dusting of dark hair and that sexy full-sleeve tattoo that has become one of my favorite sights in the world. "Now take off your shirt and your bra," he orders softly. "I want to play with your nipples while I fuck your pussy with my mouth."

"Oh, well, *that'll* make it easy not to come," I huff as I roll my eyes, but I'm already tugging his fleece and my tee over my head and reaching for the clasp on my bra.

"Beautiful. Now touch yourself," Rafe murmurs as he disposes of my jeans and panties and scoots lower on the bed, his fingers curling around my thighs, spreading them wider.

The sight of his darker, utterly masculine hands against my softer, paler skin is so erotic my nipples are already tingling, even before I cup my breasts in my palms and brush my fingers across the sensitized tips. I suck in a gasp at the same moment Rafe groans.

"Yes, just like that." He presses a reverent kiss to my thigh before shifting his gaze back to my breasts. "Now roll them for me. Make them tighter."

I obey, and he rewards me with a kiss between my legs, where I'm already hot and getting hotter with every passing second. And then his tongue finds my clit, circling me with a slow, insistent rhythm that would take me over the edge in a heartbeat if I let it.

"Please," I beg, fingers stilling as I fight the heaviness tugging sharply between my hips, demanding I come apart beneath his mouth. "I can't."

"You can," he insists, plunging his tongue deep inside me, making my pussy clench. "Keep going, Trouble. Do what I tell you to do, and I'm going to make you come like you've never come before."

Holding his gaze, I force my hands back to my breasts. After a beat, he resumes his work, staring deep into my eyes as he fucks me with his mouth, and it is by far the most intimate thing that's ever happened to me in bed. Even more intense than our sex by the beach, when every touch, every kiss carried the message that he wanted more than fucking, more than casual, making me dare to think it was okay for me to want it, too.

He brings me to the edge, again and again, taking me so close I'm gasping for breath and trembling, certain I'm going to lose control. But each time, he eases away seconds before I tumble over, leaving me lost and aching and strung so tight it feels like I'm going to spontaneously combust.

By the time he finally surges over me, claiming my mouth as he guides his cock to my entrance, I'm sobbing with relief and shaking all over. And when he whispers, "Now," into my ear as he drives inside me, I ignite.

I dig my nails into his shoulders, arch my back, and come with an intensity that's blinding. I forget who I am, where I am, what I am, only returning to my body as he brings me over again, seconds before his own release.

"Oh yes, yes," I gasp as I lock my ankles behind his ass, holding him close as he comes inside me, his pleasure making mine even sweeter.

Long moments later, he rolls onto his back, drawing me with him until I'm splayed on top of him like a very limp, sated piece of sushi atop a dollop of rice. "Damn, woman, you're beautiful. I love fucking you so much."

I hum in agreement and smile, too wasted to make rational conversation. Maybe too wasted to do anything but sleep for the foreseeable future…

I'm nearly out, floating into rosy, warm oblivion when Rafe says, "I've been thinking about your ex."

"Hmmm…why would you do that?" I ask, my words

slurred with exhaustion. "Don't think about him. He's the worst."

"He is, and that's why he needs to get out of your life and stay out." He skims his fingertips down my spine to the curve of my ass. "Do you think you could get him to meet you somewhere? Pretend you want to talk things through, get his guard down, get him talking?"

Suddenly wide awake, I lift my head, propping my arms on his chest and resting my chin on top. "I probably could. What are you thinking? Because beating the crap out of him is not an option, no matter how much I would like to smack him around a little. I haven't done anything wrong yet, and I don't want to start. I don't believe in using physical violence unless there's literally no other way to ensure your own personal safety."

"No, of course not," Rafe agrees. "I'm not a complete Cro-Magnon person, you know. I have layers."

I grin, threading my fingers through his crisp chest hair. "Yes, you do. And I wouldn't say you were a Cro-Magnon at all. I just understand that Jordan inspires insanity in otherwise reasonable people."

"But he's the crazy one," Rafe says, brushing my hair over my shoulder. "Either crazy or a compulsive liar. Either way, he's bound to contradict himself on tape. You make him feel comfortable enough, he might even confess why he staged this attack on you in the first place."

Nibbling my lip, I ask, "But any video I obtained like that wouldn't stand up in court, would it? Something I sneakily recorded without his knowledge?"

"I'm not sure, but you don't need it to stand up in

court, you just need to turn the tide, introduce enough doubt into people's minds that they stop cancelling your speaking engagements and keep buying your books."

I blink, thoughts racing. "And if I introduce enough doubt, Jordan might decide this isn't worth his time or effort and move on to his next evil scheme, hopefully with his reputation sufficiently damaged to make it harder for him to do this to someone else."

His lips curve as he studies me in the dim light, staying silent for so long I start to feel twitchy. "What?" I ask, nose wrinkling. "You're staring at me."

"You're nice to stare at. And I like that you want to keep this from happening to someone else. You're a softer touch than you let on, Trouble."

"Yeah, well don't tell anyone," I grumble. "Usually only family gets the soft stuff."

His smile drops away, replaced by an expression so intense it makes it hard to breathe. "Thanks for telling me the things you did. For letting me in."

"Ditto." I lean in to press a kiss to his lips before pulling back to gaze into his soft eyes with a smile. "Now tell me more about this scheme of yours. When and where, and am I wearing a wire because I've always wanted to wear a wire."

He scoffs. "They make cameras smaller than the tip of your pinkie finger these days, Haverford. Get with the times."

"No, I refuse," I say, grinning. "There's a reason I don't have a smartphone and stay off the Internet as much as possible. The times are exhausting. That's why technology doesn't work in any of my books. It is the enemy."

"Not this time." He rolls me beneath him as he kisses my neck. "This time it's going to be your friend."

He starts to detail his plan, but soon one kiss becomes two, and then three, and then he's moving inside me again, making me see stars brighter than anything visible in the sky. Afterward, we grab water in the kitchen and start the oven to warm up a frozen pizza, sleep banished by sex and scheming.

As we sit at his table, burning our fingertips and tongues on molten cheese, I feel happier than I have in ages. Even if our plan fails, and I can't get Jordan off my case without going to court, I have so many things to look forward to. I have days, weeks, months of getting to know this man, uncovering his mysteries, relishing his company, discovering his secrets... Finishing the job of falling in love with him because what else can I do?

Even if it's crazy, he makes me believe the fall is real.

Real, and completely worth the risk.

CHAPTER 22

*From the texts of Carrie Haverford
and Emma Haverford Hunter*

Carrie: Hey, Em… You awake?

Emma: Yes. Battling the books for this quarter.
So far, they're winning.

Carrie: Ugh. Numbers. How awful for you. I'm sorry.

Emma: Thank you. I know you understand my pain.
It would have been nice if someone in our family had a
solid math gene to toss into the mix somewhere. It's
nice that everyone's good at communicating and has an
ear for languages, but numbers are a distressingly large
part of everyday life.

Carrie: They are. And I'm sorry I can't help you with them.
The best I can do is leave you in peace and wait to pester you later.

Emma: No! No! Pester me now! Please, anything to give me an excuse to go eat ice cream while Dylan's sleeping.

Carrie: Is he trying to come between you and your ice cream?
If so, I can arrange to rough him up when I get home tomorrow.

Emma: No, he's trying to help me stay away from sugar a couple nights a week the way I promised my OB I would, but that's neither here nor there. Where are you?! Why aren't you coming home until tomorrow? Are you with the guy Mom saw you with tonight?

Carrie: WHAT? What did she say?

Emma: Not much, just that you were out with a guy and you looked really happy, so she didn't want to interrupt you to say hello. She was weirdly close-lipped about it all.

Carrie: That is weird...
And kind of nice...

Emma: Yeah, she seemed to approve. Is this guy a

lawyer who drives a Bentley? You know that's Mom's dream son-in-law.

Carrie: No, he's nothing like that. But he's one of the good ones. No doubt.

Emma: So you've been seeing him for a while, huh? And lying to your pregnant sister about it?

Carrie: I didn't lie.
I just…fudged the truth.

Emma: Ooo, fudge. That sounds good, too.
I think I have everything I need to make peppermint fudge in the pantry.
Tell me all your dirty fudging secrets while I go check.

Carrie: I don't have any secrets, at least not any I can talk about right now.
But I do have a couple of questions…
About relationships…

Emma: YOU JUST USED THE R WORD! I can't believe it!
Omg, are you getting serious with this person?

Carrie: I think I am. I think *we* are.
He wants to give the couple thing a try, too.

Emma: That's wonderful!
Assuming he's not an asshole. He's not an asshole, is he?

I mean, not that we can ever really know at the beginning, when everything is hearts and flowers, but you're not getting any icky vibes, right?

Carrie: No, I'm not getting icky vibes. And I think we know more in the beginning than we let on. At least, I usually do. Looking back, I always knew Jordan was a bad bet. I should never have taken him on as a mentee, let alone a boyfriend. He was way too focused on himself to ever get to know me.

Emma: But that was part of why you chose him, right? Because you knew he would never be anything more than the man of the moment?

Carrie: Yes, wise one. Of course, that's why.
That's why I started shacking up with this new guy, too, because I didn't think he was the type who would ever become anything more. But now he has. He's actually an amazing person with a big heart. He's just been afraid to use it.

Emma: Sounds familiar, huh?

Carrie: It does…
Which leads me to one of my questions…
Do you think people who have so much in common—especially issues and fears and broken places in common—can make love work?

Emma: Oh my…

I'm tearing up a little, Carrie. I honestly am.
First the R word and now the L word.
I didn't think I would ever see the day.

Carrie: Yeah, well... Like I said, he's special.

Emma: I'm so happy!!!
You deserve special, especially after all this crap with
Jordan.
I hate him, by the way. Fresh hate rises inside me every
time a Google alert pops up in my inbox about this
ridiculous scandal. I can't believe the balls on this guy,
the huge, nasty, hairy, entitled, delusional balls.

Carrie: I'm actually working on a plan to crush those
balls, but let's get back to that in a second. You have to
answer my question first!
What do you think?
Is it possible to make it work with someone who's
glitching in the same places you're glitching?

Emma: Well, we're not computer programs, love, so
neither of you is glitching. You're dealing with pain and
the consequences of being human. And the fact that
you've both struggled with some of the same issues
could be something that draws you closer together.
Being understood is a powerful thing.

Carrie: It is. You're totally right.
So...why am I still afraid?

Emma: Because giving up control and letting yourself fall for someone is scary as hell. Because there's no safety net. Because there's a very real chance that you'll crash and burn and that the pain of losing someone you love will make the pain of being betrayed by a guy you used to bang seem silly and small in comparison?

Carrie: Yup. That's exactly it.
Shit.
Thanks for reminding me, you sadist.

Emma: You didn't need reminding, but you do have to face the Risk Monster. You have to face it, tell it that you see it there, snarling and growling and threatening to rip your guts out, but that you're going into the relationship cave anyway. That you've consciously made the choice to walk out on the love tightrope. By acknowledging the fear, you hold it at arm's length, where it can't get under your skin and make you do crazy things like look down.

Carrie: So many metaphors in there…

Emma: Yeah, well, I'm a winemaker, not a writer.

Carrie: No seriously. I'm confused.
Am I in a cave or on a tightrope?

Emma: It doesn't matter! You know what I mean. And I know you've got what it takes to fight all the monsters, spelunk all the caves, and get across that tightrope and safely to where you want to go.

And if this guy is as great as you say he is, then he'll be right there by your side.

Or maybe in front or behind, in the case of the tightrope.

That's not really a side-by-side situation.

Carrie: True that.

Emma: So when do I get to meet Mr. Special?

Carrie: Um…soon. I think.
As long as you promise not to freak out.

Emma: Why would I freak out?

Carrie: No reason…

Emma: Are you fudging again?

Carrie: No, I'm withholding. And now I'm changing the subject.
Do you still have that black sundress with the V-neck in front, the one that shows cleavage but not too much cleavage?
And would you mind if I borrowed it for the shelter event?

Emma: I do and of course you can borrow it. I'm not wearing anything that shows my boobs at the moment.

I'm trying to wean Mercy before I get any further along in this pregnancy and that's easier if she can't see the givers of the goods.

Carrie: She's still not psyched about formula, huh?

Emma: No, she's not. And I would keep nursing her, but my doctor said it could put this pregnancy at risk since I'm of advanced maternal age, yada yada, so…
We're doing what we have to do.
Speaking of, what's your plan to crush Jordan's balls?
You have to tell me that, if you're not going to dish the dirt on new guy and why I'm going to freak out when I meet him.

Carrie: I'm going to get Jordan on tape confessing his evil. Even if it won't hold up in court, it will hold up in the court of public opinion, which is at least half the battle.

Emma: So are you going to call him?
Try to get him talking while you record the conversation?

Carrie: No, I invited him to be my date for the event tomorrow night.

Emma: WHAT?!

Carrie: He's driving up from San Francisco. We're going to go wine tasting at a few places, then hit the event, where I will ply him with more booze. He's never been able to handle his liquor, so... *fingers crossed*

Emma: But how did you get him to agree to come? And is this safe? He's clearly a horrible person, Carrie. What if he realizes what you're up to and gets violent?

Carrie: Jordan isn't a physical kind of guy. He's a lying, scheming weasel. And he thinks he's coming up here to get me to sign paperwork giving him royalty share rights for the novel I wrote while we were together. He'll be on his best behavior until I sign on the dotted line.

Emma: Which you're NEVER going to do, right?

Carrie: Hell, no. I'm going to get his confession on tape and tell him to go eat about a pound of dog shit and die.

Emma: That would be a fitting end for him.

Carrie: Indeed.

Emma: All right, well, be careful, okay? And let me know if you want me there for backup. Dylan and I have a dinner scheduled with some of his brewery connections, but I can send him off alone if I have to.

Carrie: Thanks, but there's no need. I'm going to have backup.

Emma: Mr. Special?

Carrie: Maybe…

Emma: Good for him. I like him already.
Fingers crossed for you, babes, and wishing you
good luck.

From the texts of Carrie and
Renee Haverford

Carrie: Hey, Renee. Thanks for keeping the thing with
Rafe and me quiet.
We wanted to wait to tell Emma and the rest of the
family.
So yeah…
I appreciate your discretion.

Renee: Of course. It's your business, Caroline.
I'm just glad you've found someone who makes you
smile like that.
I've missed that smile.

Carrie: Thanks, Mom. That means a lot to me.

Renee: And you mean a lot to me. I hope you know that.
Emma and I had a talk yesterday. About the past and the
three of us…
And well, I'm sorry if I've harped more than I've

praised. I just worry, and when I worry, I nag, but I'm going to try to do better. I really am. Kip is helping me get into daily meditation. It's helping me keep anxiety at arm's length and focus on the things that really matter

Carrie: Kip, huh? Was that the smoking old hippie you were with at the steakhouse?

Renee: Yes. He is smoking, isn't he?
And so wise. And he makes me laugh!

Carrie: Sounds like a good combo. I hope it works out.

Renee: You, too. As long as Rafe keeps you smiling like that, I'm on board.
And it would be so cute for the kids.
They'd be double first cousins!

Carrie: LOL! Jesus, mom, slow down. Rafe and I just started dating exclusively. We're a long way from giving you grandchildren.

Renee: That's what Emma thought a year ago and now look at her.
But no rush. Just breathe, relax, and live the moment.
It's all we've got, right?

Carrie: Yes, alien pod-person who has taken over my stressed-out mother's body, it is all we've got. But thanks for the reminder. Talk to you soon.

Renee: Maybe we can grab lunch with Mercy sometime next week.

Carrie: Sounds good. Thanks again, Mom.

Renee: I love you, Caroline. No thanks needed.

Carrie: Love you, too.

CHAPTER 23

CARRIE

*I*t's starting to feel like luck is on my side. Like the winds are shifting and good fortune is filling my sails.

But though good luck is always appreciated, it's not something you can count on.

An ounce of preparation is worth a bucket of luck, so I'm determined to do everything possible to ensure Operation Douchebag Dupe goes off without a hitch.

I spend Friday morning dashing back to Emma's to grab my toiletries and the dress she promised I could borrow—stopping by to hug my mom, who is still in an amazing new headspace, and Mercy, who is still adorable, on my way back to the car—then hitting the drugstore for beautifying supplies, the salon for a re-purpling, and the big box store off the highway, where they're running a special on tiny surveillance cameras.

I'm troubled that surveillance cameras are a purchase common enough to be thrown in an average shopper's cart along with bulk toilet paper and a bargain rotisserie chicken, but I don't have time to ponder this sad comment on humanity.

I'm too busy dealing with one awful human, in particular.

Jordan is a tricky bastard, who's good a smelling a rat. This isn't going to be easy, and it almost certainly won't be quick.

"What if I run out of recording space before he gives up the goods?" I ask, trying not to fidget as Rafe fastens my cicada broach—now with an itty-bitty camera glued in between its antennae—in place on my dress. "I could wait to start recording until he's had a few, but with my luck, that means he'll give a super villain monologue confession five minutes into the date, and I'll miss it."

Rafe's lips curve. "I hope he does. The sooner that fucker spills his guts, the sooner you can ditch him and come drink beer and pet dogs with me."

"So you think I should start recording as soon as we meet up at the first winery?"

"Definitely. Turn the camera on a few minutes before you pull up so I can text you if I'm having trouble picking up the feed. But there shouldn't be any problems. You're coming in clear now, and I bypassed the default settings so we're recording straight to my hard drive and I've got plenty of RAM."

"You do, huh?" I bite my bottom lip as his fingers brush the curve of my breast while getting the placement of the pin just right. "You have all the RAM I need?"

"All the RAM you need and more, baby." His fingers

tease beneath the neckline of my borrowed dress, making my nipples pull tight before he steps away. "But no time for ramming now. You're ready, and you need to get your fine ass on the road."

My breath rushes out. "But there will be time later, right? When we're celebrating victory? Because this isn't a terrible plan that's going to blow up in my face?"

Rafe sobers. "No, it's not a terrible plan, and it's not going to blow up in your face. But if it does, I'll be there to help with the fallout. I'll have eyes on you the entire time."

I press my lips together and nod. "Thanks."

"My pleasure." He leans in, kissing my forehead. "Now go show this jerk what a mistake it was to fuck with a woman who's out of his league."

With a last bracing breath, I head down the stairs and out into the sunny late afternoon, feeling reasonably confident.

But by the time I get to the Gloria winery—an old-fashioned adobe building perched on the edge of a sweeping vineyard not far from the shelter—I'm no longer sure I'm out of Jordan's league. I've got truth on my side, yes. But he's managed to lie his way onto the moral high ground, damage my career, and call my credibility into question with people I respect, all with nothing more than a few racy pictures and a strategic plan for chipping away at my livelihood, piece by piece.

"But you have a hidden camera," I whisper to my reflection as I apply a fresh coat of lipstick. "And he will not suspect the hidden camera because you're going to put on the performance of your life for this tool, Caroline. This is not the time for doubting the plan."

I snap the lid back onto my lipstick, cheeks flushing as pink as my lips when I remember someone is listening to me talk to myself.

But before I can assure Rafe I'm fine and only borderline crazy, a long, dark smudge in the rearview mirror catches my eye. Even before I focus in on his face, I know it's Jordan—who else would wear black jeans and a vintage smoking jacket in ninety-degree heat?

Ignoring the contempt that flashes through my chest, I force a serene expression onto my face. With one last plea to the gods for luck, I step out of the driver's seat and slam the door behind me, turning to face the slimeball oozing across the pebbled drive.

"Hey." Jordan lifts his lightly fuzzed chin, his eyes unreadable behind his dark, reflective glasses. "You look nice."

I cross my arms slowly, fighting the caustic words clawing their way up my throat. Words won't hurt this man. I need cold hard facts and evidence, which I'm only going to get if I can convince him to let down his guard.

So I nod and say, "Thank you, you look...warm."

His lips curve into a self-deprecating smile I used to think was sincere. "You know me. Can't resist a chance to get dressed up in the smoking jacket. I'm looking forward to meeting your new friends."

I know, right? Because they're totally going to LOVE the

guy who leaked nude pictures of me to the press and is doing his damnedest to ruin my life!

But once again, I bravely resist calling him on his bullshit—according to him, he has "no idea" how those pictures ended up on TMZ—and tip my head toward the winery's entrance. "Me, too. But first, drinks. You up for some Zin? They have great big reds here."

"Totally," Jordan says, but when I start toward the building, he stops me with an arm propped on the Mini Monster's roof. He reaches up, tugging off his glasses, pinning me with an earnest gaze. "I'm glad you called, Carrie. Seriously. I know we can make this right, put the ugliness of the past few weeks behind us, and get back to being good friends."

I nod, jaw loose, though I'm practically biting my tongue in half behind my teeth. "I agree. There's no reason we can't settle this like grown-ups."

He smiles, seeming to buy my "let's make a deal" act hook, line, and sinker. But I learned the hard way that Jordan isn't always what he seems. If I have a scheme, he probably has a bigger, meaner scheme already lurking in the shadows, ready to drag my scheme behind the gym, beat it up, and steal its lunch money.

I'll have to tread lightly and choose my moment, and my next move, carefully.

"But first, we drink." Clutching my tiny purse in one hand, I lightly punch his bicep with the other. "I want to see if you can tell the difference between a warm weather and a cold weather Zin without using the cheat sheet."

"I'm up for that challenge." The hint of innuendo in

his voice makes my stomach turn. Surely not even *he* can be sufficiently deluded to think we'll ever be more than friends again.

Though, who knows? He clearly thinks a lot of himself, and a ton of women go back to the men who hurt them for one reason or another.

But that was never me, and it's even less me these days, now that I'm learning what it feels like to be with a man who has my back. Who makes me feel safe, even when he's pinning me to a rock at the edge of the world and fucking my brains out, and who is making me think that maybe happy endings aren't just for the stories I write.

That maybe, just maybe…

As I slip into the winery, I glance over my shoulder, gaze skimming the parking lot and the vineyards beyond. I can't see where Rafe is hiding, but I don't doubt that he's out there somewhere. Just like he promised. He's a man who keeps his promises, and I'm a woman who's ready to put her past behind her.

Courage cranked up to the max, I join Jordan at the bar, smiling at him as I tell the host behind the counter, "We'll have the ultimate side by side tasting, please. All ten wines and the port."

CHAPTER 24

RAFE

I'm in hell.

It's hell, sitting here in the parking lot, watching my girl from afar, seeing Carrie flirt with the human shit stain who set off a bomb in the middle of her life. When he rests a hand lightly on her waist—clearly emboldened by the wine he's slugged back so far—I grit my teeth so hard it sends pain flashing through my jaw.

But I don't doubt that the plan is going to work.

The douchebag is already loosening up, saying things he shouldn't while putting his hands in places they no longer belong. And Carrie is playing it perfectly, offering enough encouragement to keep him talking while making it clear she won't be an easy sell this time around. She's gorgeous, clever, and aloof, and Jordan is clearly relishing the chase.

Or the *hunt*, I suppose, in his case.

He's a predator, this one, a fact I hope Carrie's

keeping in mind as she leads him onto a secluded observation deck high above a valley peppered with gnarled old grapevines. Yes, there are people inside the tasting room, and I could be out of the Jeep I borrowed from Tristan and across the parking lot in two minutes, but two minutes would be a minute and fifty-five seconds too late to prevent Jordan from tossing Carrie over the edge of the railing to her death.

Logically, I know this guy isn't *that* type of monster —he's slimy and deceptive, not a brute with rage issues —but logic isn't my strongest suit right now.

There's something happening inside of me, a seismic shift.

Just a few weeks ago, this rock spinning through time and space was my oyster. Every obstacle, every disappointment, trial, and setback, was nothing but a blip on my irritation radar. I was above it all, coasting along without a care, wearing my freedom like a badge of honor.

And then she happened.

She slunk in like a cat burglar and cracked my code, disabling my defenses as she reached in to steal my heart.

Except she didn't steal it.

She woke it up. Woke *me* up.

She made me realize how good it can feel to let go and let yourself get close to another person. She makes me simultaneously happier and more terrified, than I've been in a decade, but I wouldn't go back to being asleep for anything in the world. My freedom wasn't freedom; it was numbness. It was a coward's choice, a cop out. A solution hatched by a kid too young to know what to do with the pieces of his broken heart.

But I'm not a kid anymore. I'm a grown man ready to do whatever it takes to keep the woman I'm falling for safe, even if it means sitting here and stewing in my own stress instead of getting out and punching Jordan repeatedly in the face.

He's not going to hurt her. At least, not physically. She swore he's never given any indication that he would raise a hand to her, let alone push her off a deck.

My fear is irrational, and so I force my ass to stay glued to the hot leather seat, wishing I could turn on the air conditioning, but knowing an idling vehicle will attract more attention. And the air might keep me from hearing every word, every breath, every soft sigh as Carrie leans against the porch railing and says, "Seriously, it's so beautiful here. I might never go back to the city."

Jordan laughs as his palm makes circles at the small of her back. "You? Out here full time? I mean, I know you love wine, but this place is rural as fuck."

"But it's charming." She lifts a bare shoulder and lets it fall. "And I feel safe here. Most of these people are too busy making wine or drinking wine to have any time for idle gossip...or watching TMZ."

Jordan visibly tenses and my jaw locks tight in response. It's the first time Carrie's mentioned the leaked pictures or anything scandal-related. She's been keeping things light and friendly, but obviously they can't stay that way.

I just hope she's made the right call.

I narrow my eyes, cursing myself for not bringing binoculars so I could get a better look at Jordan's stupid face.

"Yeah...about that..." He pauses for a long beat, making my heart pump faster. "I truly have no idea how those pictures made it to the media. I hope you know I would never do that to you."

"I don't, sadly." Carrie sounds more bummed than angry. "You hacked into my computer and peppered my presentation with nude pictures. And you knew I was giving a talk to middle school kids. Why shouldn't I believe you're capable of leaking those same images to the press?"

Jordan shakes his head. "I'm telling you, Carrie, I never—"

"I had to sign a bunch of little boys' arms, Jordan," she cuts in. "All these twelve-year-old kids with manic lights in their eyes wanted me to sign their arms because they hadn't brought money for books but wanted a memento of the first time they saw boobs."

He snorts. "No way. They didn't say that."

"They didn't have to say it," she says, laughing with him, though I know she didn't find the situation amusing in the slightest. "I knew what they were thinking. I know twelve-year-olds, dude. I write for them. In some way I *am* them. I'm basically a twelve-year-old trapped in a grown-up's body."

"But that's one of the things I like about you," Jordan says as he takes another sip of Chardonnay. "You still know how to play like a kid. To create like one. It's magical."

She shakes her head. "So, if you like me so much, why did you do it? Why embarrass me like that? I want to understand, I really do, but you need to help me."

He sighs. "You don't want to understand. You want me to go away."

"If that's true, why invite you up here to talk?"

"To seduce me into doing things the way you want them done." He lifts a hand, skimming his finger across her shoulder and down her arm. "And it'll probably work. Because I'm crazy about you..." He cocks his head, adding in a voice that's softer and sharper at the same time, "That's why, Carrie. You can't break a man's heart and expect him to walk away without looking back."

"Without getting revenge, you mean?"

He shakes his head. "I wasn't trying to get revenge. I just..."

Biting down on my lip, I cross my fingers and silently will the man to confess already, to open his pretentious, entitled mouth and let the truth come out.

"Just...?" Carrie prods, a wistfulness in her tone that makes it seem like she understands where he's coming from. Or that she wants to understand, if only he'll open up and let her in.

"You're doing great," I murmur, wishing she could hear me.

She's got him on the hook, now all she has to do is reel him in...

Slow and steady. Don't spook him, but don't let the line go slack, either.

"I just..." He exhales, and I lean forward in my seat.

"I wanted you to feel the way I felt when you had my contract cancelled."

I pump a fist in the air. "That's right," I say, a smile spreading across my face. "Sing, motherfucker. Get it all off your chest."

"I wanted you to feel exposed and ashamed," he continues, head hanging in a weak imitation of penitence. "I was so angry, I wasn't thinking straight, or I wouldn't have done it that day. I forgot the group was so young. I thought it was another high school talk."

"And that would have been okay?" Carrie asks, incredulous. "You violated my trust in the worst way, Jordan. And I'd done nothing to deserve it."

"You violated the trust I had in you, too, Carrie," he says, clearly determined to paint himself as a victim. "That book was my baby, and you took it away from me. You ripped it out of my hands and said it wasn't mine, that it had never been mine to begin with. Can you imagine what that feels like?"

"Books are not babies. Only babies are babies," she says, voice rising. "And if that book *were* a baby, and you'd been the only one taking care of it, it would have died from neglect. I refuse to apologize for taking credit for my own work or for insisting on my rights as a contributor. You asked for my help, I gave it, and I ended up giving more than you did. Honestly, I was being generous to offer to let you have your name on it at all."

Jordan sets his wine down on the porch railing hard enough for Carrie's mic to pick up the clink. "You had no right to that story! The world and the characters were mine."

"That's like saying you should get credit for making the shepherd's pie because you brought over carrots and potatoes." She sets her wine down beside his with a matching clink. "You didn't make the pie; you gathered a few raw ingredients. That story would never have become something edible, let alone delicious, without me. Surely, you know that. Deep down, in whatever part of you isn't completely deluded by your own narcissism."

Jordan's hands tighten into fists, sending a rush of unease through my chest.

"And let's talk about the other claims you're making." Carrie turns her back on him as she paces back toward the entrance to the winery, a decision that has me reaching for the door handle and wrapping my fingers around it.

You don't turn your back on someone with his hands balled into fists.

You keep that fucker in sight so you know when to duck.

"If you hit her, I swear to fucking god..." I grit out with a shake of my head. My gut is screaming for me to get over there and put myself between Carrie and the man glaring daggers into her back, but she's close to exposing all his bullshit, recording every word for the world to see.

I curse beneath my breath as I remember the location of the camera. It's pinned to the front of her dress. If she doesn't turn around, she's not going to get

Jordan's reaction on tape. She'll get audio, but not visual.

"Turn around, Carrie," I mutter. "Turn around."

"You say you deserve a share of the royalties for my latest book," she continues, "the one I'm finishing right now, far away from you, and the latest in a series I've been writing for years. That's completely ridiculous, and anyone with a brain knows it. I was hitting the bestseller list long before you latched onto me like a blood-sucking leech, and I will continue to do so when you're out of my life for good."

"Fuck you," he growls, all pretense of nostalgia for their failed love gone from his voice. "You're a fucking bitch."

"Maybe so," Carrie agrees, still not turning to face him. "If a bitch is a woman who refuses to be bullied or blackmailed, then I suppose I am. But the fact remains that you, Jordan Jakes, are a fraud, a liar, and a criminal. Revenge porn is against the law in California. You realize that, right?"

"You're the criminal." He takes a menacing step closer to Carrie that she can't see. "You stole from me and made me look like a fucking fool in front of our entire community."

"Turn around, Trouble," I say, fighting the urge to shout it.

Carrie laughs, the light, easy sound making Jordan's face flush redder. "You didn't need help making yourself look pathetic, buddy. You did that all by yourself." She reaches out, caressing a daisy sprouting from a pot on the empty picnic bench beside her. "And you're going to look like even more of a fool when you lose this lawsuit. Considering you haven't been able to get a single project published on your own—or finished, for that matter—I seriously doubt a judge is going to rule in your favor."

She sighs happily. "And then I'm going to make you pay my lawyer fees and counter sue you for every dime in your pathetic bank account, just to teach you a lesson about treating people with respect. Doesn't that sound like fun?"

Jordan lunges forward, and I explode out of the Jeep, sprinting across the parking lot, fists pumping as I hit the grass on the other side and haul ass toward the deck.

But no matter how fast I am, I won't be fast enough.

I'm still halfway across the lawn, and Jordan already has his arm locked around Carrie's throat, lifting her off her feet as he drags her toward the edge of the deck.

My breath rasps fast in my chest, seconds stretching into endless, terror-thickened minutes as what I feared gets insanely close to becoming a reality.

I watch one of the tasting room hosts—a man in a blue button-down with a messy red bun—burst through the door in slow motion, arms outstretched and fingers spread, shouting for Jordan to "Stop! Put her down!"

I have time to notice the way Jordan's too-long hair blows into his eyes as he turns to glance over the side of the deck, the way Carrie's face flushes and her lips open wide in an attempt to suck in a breath. I have time to realize how small she looks next to him, something I hadn't noticed when she was putting that creep in his place like a fucking boss.

And in that second, I know that I'm going to hit him. I'm going to smash my fist into his face hard enough to lift him off the ground. Let's see how he enjoys having someone bigger and stronger take advantage of him, that psycho piece of shit.

I vault over the deck railing, not bothering to side-step the three feet to go through the gate, and sprint the last ten feet separating me from the struggle. It's clear by now that Jordan isn't going to try to toss Carrie over the edge—he's already relaxing his hold on her neck, apparently having decided murder in front of witnesses isn't a good idea—but that doesn't make a difference to me.

He put his fucking hands on her. That's enough.

More than enough.

I grip him by the shoulders, ripping him away from Carrie. I'm drawing back my arm, ready to shove my fist into his gut, when familiar hands circle my bicep.

"Don't! He's not worth it." Carrie wraps herself around me, and I turn to pull her into my arms, hugging her tight, so fucking glad she's okay.

"You sure?" I ask, smoothing her hair from her forehead.

"Yes," she says, nodding firmly. "But thank you."

"I'm going to sue," Jordan shouts. "That's fucking assault."

"I didn't touch you," I say, shaking my head as I scowl at him. Seriously, is this guy for real?

"Assault is the threat of violence." Jordan rakes a hand through his hair as he lifts his chin. "You threatened me. Clearly."

I'm about to give him an earful about being a hypocrite of the lowest, sleaziest order, but the tasting room guy beats me to it.

"And you were *strangling* your girlfriend," he says, shoving open the gate leading off the deck and pointing a finger toward the parking lot. "Get out of here. Now. Before we call the police. There are cabs at the end of the drive." He hesitates, expression softening as he shifts his attention Carrie's way. "Unless you want us to call the police for you, ma'am. Do you want to press charges?"

"No." Carrie shakes her head. "I just want him to go and stay gone."

"You can't do this," Jordan seethes, but thankfully he starts moving toward to the gate. "You can't make me go away. You're not as smart as you think you are, Carrie. Just wait until we're in court. My lawyer is a pit bull. He's going to make sure I get everything I want, and then some."

"She's got you on video, asshole," I say, relishing the dumbstruck look that flashes across his face.

"Including you rushing me from behind," Carrie says. "The windows reflected everything, like a mirror. So unless you want me to release footage of you assaulting me to the press *and* the authorities, I suggest you withdraw your suit, apologize publicly for leaking the photos, and stay the hell out of my life. Moving would be nice, too. A state away. Or two. Canada would be good."

"Don't put that on Canada, babe," I say with mock disappointment. "They don't deserve this shit stain."

Carrie laughs, triggering a scowl from Jordan. His lips part, but I cut him off before he can stick his foot in his mouth again.

"You're done." I jerk my chin toward the parking lot. "Start walking and don't look back."

He starts to speak, but again, I'm too fast for him.

"Huh-uh." I point to the road. "Leave. Now. Or leave with my foot in your ass, kicking you to the curb."

But the fool clearly doesn't know when to shut up. He takes a breath, and I launch into motion. The speed with which he scrambles away would be funny if he hadn't had his arm locked around Carrie's throat two minutes ago. So instead of laughing, I chase the idiot down the driveway and into a cab. Only when he's safely inside, flipping me the bird from behind the window, do I let myself laugh.

And laugh and laugh, because nothing hurts a bully more than realizing he's a fucking joke.

By the time I make it back to the winery, Carrie is waiting for me at the end of the walk, holding a bottle of wine wrapped in purple tissue paper. "For you," she says, holding it out to me. "A 'thank you for helping me get my life back' present."

"Thanks, but I don't want wine," I say.

"What do you want?" she asks, lips curving as her palm slides up my chest.

"Just this, Trouble." I bend low, claiming her lips for a long, slow, relieved kiss before pulling away. "Just you."

CHAPTER 25

CARRIE

*J*didn't go to my high school prom.

I went to a concert with my girlfriends, instead, secure in the knowledge that I wasn't missing a damned thing. Screw high school rites of passage, and screw high school. I was already a million miles away in my mind.

I've never regretted the choice, and I don't regret it now, but I do love to dance, and for the first time I think it might be nice to sway in a man's arms all night.

This man's arms in particular...

"I wish we'd danced at Emma's wedding," I say, studying Rafe's face in the warm glow of the exposed bulbs crisscrossing the air above us.

The open area beside the horse paddocks has been transformed into an old-fashioned wooden dance floor, with the band on an elevated platform not far from the feed troughs. Tables swathed in red cloth surround the dancing zone, giving tired patrons and pups a place to relax with a drink—or a bowl of water—in between cutting a rug or playing fetch on the hillside. Closer to the main building, cooks from three local restaurants are filling the air with incredible smells, wineries are pouring wine, breweries are showcasing their beers, and Tristan is raking in the dough needed to cover the shelter's unexpected summer costs.

It's been an amazing night, a complete success, and I truly can't remember the last time I felt so light. So happy. So filled with gratitude and hope for the future.

Rafe shakes his head. "Nah. Dancing at the wedding wouldn't have been a good idea."

"Why not?" I ask, brows lifting.

"The chemistry would have given us away." He wraps his arm tight around me as he spins us in a circle, lifting my feet off the floor before setting me down with a skill that makes it clear this isn't his first time making a woman swoon on the dance floor. "Our family would have taken one look at the sizzle and staged an intervention."

I laugh as I glance over my shoulder to where his brother is helping pull taps at the beer station. "What about Tristan? You think he'll try to shut us down?"

He shakes his head. "Tristan knows when to let life take its natural course. Which reminds me of something I've been meaning to ask you…"

"What's that?"

"It's about my gear shift, actually."

I grin. "One of my favorite topics."

"Good to hear, but..." He trails off, spinning us closer to the edge of the dance floor before adding in a softer voice, "It's about what you said at the wedding. About how humans aren't designed to make the couple thing work long term."

"I remember," I say, my smile fading.

"So...I guess I'm wondering if you really meant that."

I press my lips together as I search his eyes, looking for clues as to what he's hoping to hear. But in the end, it doesn't matter. My truth is what matters, even if it's scary to say out loud. "The idea of finding The One has always seemed weird to me. Allegedly there's this person out there, this singular, phenomenal person who will be everything we'll ever need—our best friend, our lover, our partner, our confessor, our missing piece..."

I pull in a breath, letting it out slowly. "I don't think any one person can or *should have to be* all those things. It's too much to put on one soul. I can be a lot of things to the people I love, but not everything, not *The One*. I would try, but I'm afraid I would fail. And if there's one thing I learned growing up, it's how much it sucks to fail at love."

"It does suck," Rafe says, understanding in his eyes. "But I would never expect you to be my everything, Carrie. I want your passion and your time. I want your trust and your body next to me in my bed, but..." He shrugs. "I like to figure out the answers to the big questions myself. And if something is missing in my life, it's something I need to go looking for inside myself, not in another person." He pulls me closer as the music shifts to a swoony ballad. "Not even the person I'm falling in love with."

My breath catches, and my eyes get mistier than they were before. "Yeah? You're falling in love with me?"

"Yeah," he confirms, the mixture of heat and heart in his gaze making my stomach flip. "But I don't want to share you. It makes me crazy to think of another man tuning your transmission, no matter how my gear shift is designed."

"I don't need any other gear shift but yours." I lean in, loving the way his powerful body feels pressed to mine. "It's just that the science used to give me comfort, you know? When love kept bottoming out on me, I could blame nature instead of myself."

"It wasn't you or nature," he says with a cocky grin. "You just hadn't met the right guy yet. You needed someone who could handle you, Trouble, keep you in line."

I laugh as I arch a brow. "Is that right? And you think you're up for the job, Slick?"

"Absolutely." His eyes sparkle with a mixture of teasing and truth. "As long as you'll do the same for me. Don't put up with any of my shit, okay?"

"I won't," I promise, sobering. "So does that mean the next time you run away, I get to send you a text telling you to get your cowardly ass back here and talk to me?"

He shakes his head. "No more running. I'm done with that. The only place I'm running is up the stairs to beat you to the bedroom, so I can be on bottom."

"You don't have to race me. I'll let you be on bottom," I say, threading my fingers into his hair. "I like you on bottom. And on top. And from behind. And in the car and up against the wall and—"

My words end in a moan as he kisses me thoroughly, deeply, pulling away seconds before the kiss gets too hot for public consumption.

"Save it for when we get home," he whispers. "Or we're leaving early."

"Fine by me. I've already had a glass of wine, petted the puppies, and filled out my raffle ticket."

He grins, and I'm struck again by how handsome he is. How clever and kind and an utter joy to spend time with. Not to mention a complete person who knows what he wants and isn't afraid to ask for it. And then there's the heroic side that's had me humming since he chased Jordan to his cab.

He's my knight in faded denim, and I can't believe I ever thought casual would be easy to pull off with him. He's already under my skin and so close to my heart I'm ready to put a key into his keeping.

I will always keep the master key for myself—my heart is mine to lock and unlock as I see fit—but I'm ready to make space for Rafe. I'm ready to know what it feels like to be that close to someone, so close that you know what they're going to do before they do it, what they'll say before the words pass their lips.

"Let's get out of here," he says at the same time I say, "Ready to go?"

We both grin. And then we make a break for the parking lot, where we abandon my car and head for Rafe's bike. Because we like the speed, the rush, and the wind in our hair, buffeting our skin as we race past the rest of the people clogging the 101 South, bound for a place where we can be alone.

Or not so alone, I think, smiling against his back, hoping we keep riding together for a long, long time to come.

CHAPTER 26

RAFE

Nine months later...

$\mathcal{I}$f at first you don't succeed, try, try again.

The mantra is ingrained in my DNA. Hunters don't quit, we don't back down, and we sure as hell don't let failure get in our way.

Failure is just another step on the road to eventual success. My dad worships at the church of Henry Ford, the man who tanked two auto companies before taking the world by storm with his Model T, and he made sure his sons all got the message: don't give up. Don't doubt yourself. And when a dream's burning a hole inside you, don't stop until you make your dream a reality.

I'm not easily discouraged, and I'm prepared to attack a problem from a different angle. But there are some things you want to get right the first time.

Things like proposing to the woman you love...

"You've got this," I mutter as I ease away from the

wall at the back of the bookstore and take my place at the end of the line of people waiting to get their book signed.

After Jordan's public confession nine months ago—and subsequent six week stay in a prison in Centinela when the state decided to press charges—Carrie's come back stronger than ever. Her fans have rallied around her and there are far more adults here than I thought there would be. I expected a certain number of parents along to chaperone their kids, but the crowd is eighty percent eighteen and over, which makes this more anxiety-provoking than I thought it would be. Making a spectacle in front of a couple dozen kids who probably won't be paying attention—grown-ups are boring to children, something my nephews taught me long ago—is one thing. Ripping my heart out and offering it to Carrie in front of witnesses who might notice what I'm doing or—God forbid—Instagram it, is something else entirely.

Not too late to abort the mission, the inner voice warns. *You could head out the back way and wait for her in the parking lot like you said you would. She never has to know you were in here.*

Instead, I stay where I am, shuffling forward as the line advances.

I worked for hours on the book clutched tight in my hand, and I'm not going to come up with a more romantic way to ask the question burning inside of me. Besides, I promised Carrie no more running, and I intend to keep that promise—today and every day that I'm lucky enough to call her mine.

Hopefully, that will be something close to forever.

I never imagined I'd be one of those guys desperate to get down on one knee, but Carrie's already so much a part of me I can hardly remember what my life was like without her. She fits into my family like she was meant to be in our lives all along, and both my parents and all my brothers adore her. We live together, play together, take our two beautiful nieces to the park together, and then go home and celebrate the fact that we have no small people depending on us to feed or diaper them and are still free to do filthy things to each other all night long.

But lately, we've also spent some time whispering softly in the fort of silence, wondering what it might be like to have a Hunter-Haverford of our own someday.

Maybe a day not too far from this day...

She's going to say yes.

I know she will. She makes me feel loved every fucking day, and I know there's nowhere else she wants to be than right here, sharing her life with me.

So why am I suddenly sweating?

By the time Carrie's blond and purple curls come into view, my palms are so slick I have to keep swapping the book from hand to hand to covertly wipe them on my jeans. And by the time I'm three people away from her table, my heart is punching a hole in my chest, my throat is locked tight, and I can't remember a single thing I planned to say.

Shit!

I had it all planned, the perfect words. I wrote them out ahead of time and read them over and over again, knowing I'm not the kind who can be trusted to whip up something pitch-perfect on the spur of the moment.

Apparently, I'm also not the kind of person who can remember shit when he's really nervous. You really do learn something new every day.

But it's too late to put this new intelligence to practical use. I'm here, stepping up to the table as a mother and her preteen daughter move to the side, watching my girl's face light up when she sees me.

As soon as my eyes meet Carrie's, I feel like the only person in the room, because this incredible woman is smiling just for me. My heartbeat slows, my throat relaxes, and when I hand over the book, my arm only shakes the tiniest bit. "Would you sign my copy, Miss Haverford?"

Her dimples pop. "Of course, Mr. Hunter. Though you didn't have to buy one, you know. I would have given you a copy free of charge. It's one of the perks of being my sexy boyfriend."

"I like those perks." I fight to keep my expression neutral as she opens the book. "But I wanted to support the author."

"That's very sweet of…" Her words trail off as she glances down, discovering the hidden compartment I carved in the pages of an old dictionary the same size as her book before dressing it in the latest Kingdom of Charm and Bone dust jacket. She laughs as she pulls the small wooden box from the hole in the pages and looks up at me, eyes dancing. "And what is this?"

"Read it." I nod toward the box.

Eyes narrowing suspiciously, but clearly enjoying

the surprise, she glances down, reading aloud the inscription etched into the wood. "Some stories shouldn't have an end. Like love stories..."

Her breath catches, and as she opens the box— slowly, carefully—I drop to one knee. I'm dimly aware of some shocked coos and squeals from behind me, but I only have eyes for Carrie. I never want to forget the look of wonder on her face, the happy tears that fill her eyes, or the way her smile bursts across her face, so dazzling I fall deeper in love with her on the spot.

"Is this for real?" She laughs, blinking fast as she swipes fingers beneath her eyes.

"As real as the heart attack I almost had waiting in line to give you that ring," I say, reaching to take her hand in mine. "I don't want this story to end, Trouble. I don't ever want to stop making memories and wishes and plans and magic with you."

Her face almost crumples, but she regains control with a sharp inhale. "Oh man, me too."

"So that's a yes?" I ask, shocked to find my own eyes beginning to sting.

"You haven't asked me yet," she says, her laughter echoed by the book lovers looking on.

"Sh-shoot," I say, editing myself just in time. I laugh and take a breath, letting the words come from the heart. "Will you marry me, Carrie Haverford? And write this love story with me for a really, really long time?"

"Yes," she whispers, eyes shining. "I will."

Not wanting to look away from her for even a second, I fumble for the ring. It takes an extra moment or two, but I finally pluck it free and slide it onto her finger.

Cheers erupt from the crowd as Carrie stands up, sliding across the top of the table into my arms. Her wrists loop around my neck and we kiss, soft and sweet and appropriately PG, but some kid from the back of the room still cries, "Ew, gross!" making everyone laugh.

Carrie and I pull apart, smiling too hard to keep kissing.

But that's okay. There will be time for kissing later. A good forty or fifty years if we're lucky.

"Will you still ride on the back of my bike when we're seventy?" I ask later, as Carrie swings onto the seat behind me.

"Totally." She grins. "So, what do we do first? Go home and celebrate in bed? Or call the family and tell them the news?"

"Bed," we answer at the same time, making her laugh. And she's so cute I can't help kissing her again, one more long, slow, sultry kiss to tide me over until we're home and I can have her every way I want her.

Every way she wants me. Every way we fit together so perfectly it's hard to believe I ever doubted there was someone out there who would have room in her heart for all of me—my strengths and weaknesses, my sharp edges and soft spots, my fearlessness and secret doubts, and everything in between.

But she does, and, standing in front of Father Pete six months later, at the edge of that windswept cliff where I first started falling hard for this woman, I have no doubt she always will.

"And do you take this man to be your lawfully wedded husband?" Father Pete asks, raising his voice to be heard over the roar of the surf and the rush of the breeze.

"I do," Carrie says with a smile, her cheeks pink from the chill.

It's only fifty degrees this October Saturday on the coast, but Carrie and I didn't want to wait any longer to seal the deal. And as far as I'm concerned, this moment is as perfect as any ever will be. In a long-sleeved white wedding dress made of antique lace, purple combat boots, and her hair pulled up in clips made of driftwood and sea glass, she is…stunning.

Breathtaking. So beautiful that when I'm finally given permission to kiss my bride, I can't resist lifting her off her feet in a bear hug and kissing her like I mean it.

But the kids here are too young to think kissing is gross, and our family and friends simply hoot and applaud, egging us on.

After pictures, in which the wedding party is grinning and windswept, we pile into our cars and caravan up the coast to the dive bar we've rented out for our reception, Carrie and I leading the way in our wedding present to each other, the big yellow Cadillac we've had our eye on since two summer's ago, with a "Just Married" sign tied to the back. Hours later, after we've visited with family and friends, cut the cake, and cranked up the jukebox, we leave her bouquet on the bar with a sign that says "Free to a Good Home," and slip out the back door, trusting fate will get it to the person who needs it.

While the people we love party on, we go cruising on the back roads until we find the perfect place for some wedding night parking under the stars. And it is perfect, wild and sweet, just like my bride, and as we lie together after, I can't help asking, "Is it wrong to be this excited about locking down your pussy for life?"

She hums in amusement. "Is it wrong that I want to knit your dick a little sweater as thanks for all the good times he gives me?"

"Oh, he'd like a sweater." I hug her closer, kissing the top of her head as we snuggle under the fleece blanket. "A pink one like you made for Mercy."

Carrie snorts and squeezes my thigh. "Okay. I'll do that. With sparkles and everything."

"You're good to him. And to me."

She looks up at me, eyes shining in the moonlight. "And I always will be, baby."

"Me, too," I promise, never having meant any words more. Except maybe these, "Can I take you home and carry you over the threshold now, Mrs. Hunter?"

"Yes, please."

So I do. I carry her through the door, up the stairs, and straight to my bed where we stay for a very, very long time.

CHAPTER 27

*A*fter sixteen months, two weeks, and three days, I'm finally at a place where I can attend a wedding without spending every second thinking about the one who got away. The one who *threw* me away when she woke up one morning, decided being with one man for the rest of her life was a fate worse than death, dropped my ring on the bedside table, and bolted as fast as her shapely legs could carry her.

Kim.

For a solid month, after she left, I wasn't worth shooting in the face. I lost weight, I lost my sense of humor, I damned near lost my will to live.

I know my brothers thought I was being a melodramatic, lovesick bastard, but Kim and I had been together since high school. I had been head over heels in love with the girl she was and the woman she'd become.

She was my future, every bit as much as my father or my brothers.

More so, if I'm honest.

Kim didn't expect me to be the calm, level-headed voice of reason all the time. Kim let me be a complete person, living in 3D. She saw every side of me—light and dark, serious and silly, dedicated and flexible, determined, and yet still sometimes so lost as to what I should do next.

I thought she was The One. I was fucking positive of it, in fact.

And when The One decides to call off your engagement and move to the other side of the world to live on a continent full of deadly fauna...

Well, it's enough to give a man a complex.

The Australian beaches have jellyfish with a sting so excruciating the pain alone is enough to *kill* a man. They have ticks whose bites can send people into anaphylactic shock, spiders with venom that causes organ failure, and massive saltwater crocodiles that can grow to nearly twenty feet long and over two thousand pounds.

Not to mention sharks. Three kinds.

"She hates sharks. I should have known she'd be back," I mutter over the rim of my beer, fighting the urge to turn and glare at the woman across the room.

Of all the bars in all the world, why did my ex and her new man have to walk into this dive in the middle of my brother's wedding reception? Right when I was proving to myself, and all my concerned family members, that I was over her and moving the fuck on?

My older brother Deacon grunts in solidarity. "You

want to get out of here?" he asks, pushing his half-finished beer away and sliding off his stool. "I'm newly retired and have nowhere to be for the first time in my life. We could hit a few bars in Santa Rosa, drink too much, get a car home, eat pancakes at three a.m."

My lips curve. "Normally I'd say yes, but I've got to be at the shelter at seven tomorrow. Someone finally agreed to adopt that domesticated buffalo, but they need to pick him up early before they head home to Mendocino. Then I've got a pair of ferrets who need medicine, and a blind cat who may or may not have diabetes—we're getting her tested. And then Zoey and I have to run numbers and place a food order before noon. Going to be a big day."

Deacon's blue eyes crinkle at the edges as he claps a hand on my shoulder. "Talking to you always makes me glad I have kids instead of pets."

I grimace. "I hear you."

"Call me if you change your mind," he says, backing toward the door. "And whatever you do, don't talk to her. Don't even look at her if you can help it."

I nod and lift a hand, though I have no intention of following my brother's advice. As soon as Kim pulls her giggling, flushed face out of her new boyfriend's asshole, I'm going to wave hello with my most relaxed smile and make it clear that I couldn't care less that she's moved on.

Then, I'll leave. Then, and only then.

I may be "the nice brother," but I still have my pride, dammit.

I take a slow, shallow sip of my beer, determined to nurse it as long as I have to when Zoey suddenly appears in front of me, wide-eyed and clearly in a panic, blocking my view of Kim and her beefy new man candy.

"Hide me," she whispers, her face going so pale the freckles dusted across her nose and cheeks stand out in stark relief. "You have to hide me. Please. Just tuck me under your jacket or a bar stool, something."

"Why? What's wrong?" I sit up straighter, doing my best to offer her cover. Zoey is my oldest employee, but she's also a good friend. If she needs to hide, I'll help her.

I can't imagine what has her so upset. She's usually the most upbeat, sunny person I know.

"This horrible person I went to college with is here," she says, scooting closer to the bar and my stool. "She made fun of me for three years, and now she's here with Bear, my ex-boyfriend, who I thought was the sweetest person in the world. But if he's with her, he's not sweet. He's awful. And she's awful, and I'm afraid if they see me I'm going to cry or faint or throw up in the middle of the dance floor."

"All right, no worries, we've got this." I ease off my stool, my own drama forgotten. "Tell me where they are. I'll be your human shield, block you from view until we get to the door, and then we'll bail. Go get a drink somewhere with no assholes in it."

Her shoulders sag and her bright blue eyes flood with gratitude. "Thank you, Tristan. So much. They're over by the window. The big guy with the fuzzy face and the girl with the platinum blond hair and a chunk of ice for a heart."

I go still, chest tightening. Surely she can't mean...

I mean, I know Kim isn't the person I thought she was, but surely she wouldn't torture a sweetheart like Zoey? "The woman in the red sweater? Black pants?"

Zoey's forehead furrows as she nods. "Yes. Why?"

"That's Kim," I blurt out.

"Kim." She frowns harder before her brows shoot up in sudden understanding. "*The* Kim? *Your* Kim?"

"Yes," I whisper. "Her picture used to be on my desk in my office."

"Well, I never go into your office," she hisses, looking distressed. "I respect your space. You're my boss."

"She came to the benefit gala with me three years in a row. Surely you met her there. Or when she used to bring me lunch?"

"No, I never saw her, Tristan," Zoey insists. "I never had a date for the gala and somehow I managed to miss the lunch visits from your evil ex-girlfriend. Believe me, if I'd known you were dating Kimberly Khan, I would have remembered it." She exhales sharply, adding beneath her breath, "And I would have quit my job, so I never had to risk running into her again."

Damn, that sounds serious. "What did she do to you?" I ask, unable to help myself.

"How many hours have you got," she grumbles, glancing over her shoulder before turning back to me with a soft yip of terror. "Oh my God, she's coming! She's coming; she's seen us. What do we do? I rode here with Violet and I can tell she's not ready to leave." Zoey grabs handfuls of my jacket, clinging to me with a desperation that makes my pulse race.

I look down into her panicked face and am suddenly struck by how pretty she is.

And if there's one thing I know Kim hates, it's competition. For anything—even for things she's decided she doesn't want anymore.

Trusting my gut, I lift a hand, sliding my fingers gently through Zoey's sun-streaked brown hair as I whisper, "Just go with me, okay?"

Her lips part, but before she can speak, I cover her mouth with mine, kissing her slowly, gently at first, shocked by the sizzle that races across my skin in response. Before I know it, her arms are around my neck and I'm tugging her curvy body against mine and my tongue is stroking into her sweet mouth while she gives as good as she gets, pressing closer as the kiss grows deeper, hotter.

Soon I'm hard, aching, and entertaining all sorts of inappropriate thoughts about my number one employee. Thoughts about Zoey laid out on my bed while I kiss every freckle on her body, while I taste her, tease her, make her bright eyes flash even brighter as I make her come.

I lose all awareness of time, space, or approaching exes until a familiar laugh tinkles through the air.

Zoey and I jump apart, and I turn to see Kim standing inches away, grinning up at me with an expression that says she isn't buying our act for a minute.

Only...it wasn't an act.

Well, it was when I decided to kiss Zoey. But now...

God, I don't know what that was, only that I want to do it again as soon as possible.

"Hi, Kim," Zoey says in a flat voice I've never heard from her before. "How are you?"

"I'm great. And how are you, Zoey? Still getting drunk and kissing random men at parties, I see."

"She was kissing her fiancé, actually," I find myself saying, my mouth making executive decisions before my brain can weigh in. I'm dimly aware of Zoey staring up at me with a stunned expression, but I just hug her closer and smile. "You ready to go, babe? Or do you want to grab another beer?"

"I'm r-ready to go, honey," Zoey stammers. "Good to see you, Kim."

"Totally," Kim says, sounding less confident than she did a moment before. "See you two around, then. I'm here until the New Year when Bear and I are heading back to Swan Valley for the harvest." She laughs and rolls her eyes, those eyes I used to think were the kindest, sexiest eyes in the entire world. "Weirdly enough, we're actually renting a condo close to our old place, Tristan. So, I guess we'll all be neighbors."

Inwardly I curse the cruel and heartless fates—living next door to my ex will be about as much fun as a standing date for a daily root canal—but outwardly I simply smile and say, "Guess so. See you around, neighbor."

Zoey and I head for the door, my arm around her waist, playing the happy couple while I silently wonder what fresh hell my big mouth has gotten me into this time. Me *and* Zoey. There's no easy way out of this lie.

The only way to escape with our dignity intact is to pretend to be engaged—at least until Kim and Bear go back to the land Down Under.

I do some quick calculations as I tuck Zoey into the passenger's seat of my truck and circle around to the other side—Halloween is a week away. Then roughly four and a half weeks in November, another four and a half in December...

Ten weeks.

To save face, Zoey and I are going to have to pretend to be madly in love for ten whole weeks.

Fuck...

I slide into the driver's seat and slip the key into the ignition. "I'm so sorry, Zoey. I don't know what I was thinking. I just opened my mouth and craziness came out."

"Just drive," she whispers softly. "And look happy. She's watching us through the window. We can talk more on the road."

"Gotcha." I force a smile as I reach across the truck to give Zoey's knee an apologetic squeeze, surprised again by the electricity that hums across my skin when we touch. Memories of the way her full lips felt pressed to mine, of the way she tastes—like salted strawberries and summertime—rush through my head as I pull out onto Highway One and aim the truck east, away from the coast. Zoey's been my right-hand woman for three years, and not once in that entire time has our relationship been anything but professional. I was with Kim when I hired her, but even if I'd been single, I'm not the kind of guy who hits on his employees. I would never abuse my position that way or do anything to make my staff feel uncomfortable.

Until now, asshole. Ten minutes in Kim's presence and you're already losing your shit again.

I wince at the thought but refuse to let the voice of doom prove prophetic.

I will figure a way out of this mess with my self-respect, my professional reputation, and my friendship with Zoey intact. All three mean too much to me to settle for anything less.

"I don't know about you, but I could really go for a glass of wine," Zoey says, rubbing at the backs of her eyes with her finger and thumb. "I'm not nearly tipsy enough to unpack the past fifteen minutes."

"Want to hit Locals on the square? My treat?"

"Sounds good." Zoey sighs as she leans back in her seat, her pale face captured by the moonlight streaming in through the window. She looks tired and more stressed than I've ever seen her, making me wonder all over again what the hell Kim did to her back when they were in school.

But she also looks...beautiful. Ethereal in the moonlight with her lips softly parted and her perfect profile highlighted against the night sky.

How on earth have I worked next to this woman every day for years and not noticed that her mouth is a work of fucking art? Or that she's every bit as sexy as she is sweet?

Better question—how am I going to go back to being

her boss and friend now that I know how incredible it feels to kiss her?

THE HEARTBREAKER, Tristan and Zoey's story releases May 2018.

Learn more and grab pre-order links at Lili's website: https://www.lilivalente.com/the-heartbreaker

TELL LILI YOUR FAVORITE PART

I love reading your thoughts about the books and your review matters. Reviews help readers find new-to-them authors to enjoy. So if you could take a moment to leave a review letting me know your favorite part of the story —nothing fancy required, even a sentence or two would be wonderful—I would be deeply grateful.

Thank you and happy reading!

SNEAK PEEK OF THE HEARTBREAKER

I've waited years for my drop dead sexy boss, Tristan Hunter, to notice me as something other than his right hand gal. But though his dog is deeply in love with me, Tristan and I seem doomed to the friend zone.

Until the night we kiss...

Our make out session is for the benefit of the two heartbreakers who dumped us, but very real sparks fly when his lips meet mine.

At least...they're real for me.

Yes, I've secretly dreamed of being Mrs. Hunter, but I don't know if I have what it takes to pull off a fake relationship with a man who already has my heart.

***

She's my employee, one of my best friends, my dog Luke's not-so-secret crush, and totally off limits.

So why am I suddenly unable to think of anything but Zoey Childers?

Two days into our fake engagement and I'm dying to take her to bed and show her just how real the heat could be between us. But crossing that line wouldn't just be borderline unethical—it could be lethal to our friendship.

Zoey isn't a casual fling kind of girl, and after the way things ended with my ex I don't trust my instincts when it comes to love.

I should call off this fake engagement before somebody gets hurt, but how to say "no" to something real with Zoey when every bone in my body is dying to say "yes?"

Learn more at Lili's website:
https://www.lilivalente.com/the-heartbreaker

SNEAK PEEK!

LIKE A BOSS
by Sylvia Pierce and Lili Valente

Out now!

Jack

How is it that we've invented phones advanced enough to stream movies and order groceries with a single tap, but no one can figure out how to make the subway smell less like urine?

Will scientists colonize Mars in my lifetime?

Will subways on Mars still smell like pee?

If people eat asparagus on Mars and pee on the subway, will the subway smell like pee, or asparagus?

These are the mysteries I ponder as I stare across my

mahogany desk, wondering if the guy I'm interviewing has any clue I've already voted him off the island.

"In conclusion," Brian says, "by utilizing proven Six Sigma strategies, I was able to radically streamline our core business process, eradicating inefficiencies in our product development lifecycle and increasing revenues by nine percent."

Nope. Not a clue.

"Impressive," I say. "So you're a Six Sigma guy?"

"There's no problem it can't solve, and as a broker for Seyfried and Holt, I assure you—problem-solving would become my middle name."

"What's your middle name now?" I ask. Dick move, perhaps, but I can't help myself. Seventh interview of the day, and each candidate has been as cookie-cutter as the one before. Blair was supposed to clear these guys in round one, sending me the cream of the crop.

But apparently she's looking for docile and predictable, a guy who will tow the company line and get the job done by the book.

Me? I prefer a little fire.

"Forgive me. Terrible sense of humor," I say, dialing it down. It's not this poor guy's fault I'm being blown off for lunch. No. That honor belongs to one Eleanor Seyfried, who hasn't bothered to return a single one of my texts.

Ellie Seyfried—now *there's* a problem Six Sigma can't solve.

"Tell me more about your client acquisition philosophy," I add.

I try to pay attention to Brian's answer. Honestly, I do.

But this thing with Ellie has me on edge, which is definitely *not* my standard operating procedure. Sure, she's always thrown me off my game—even when Ian and I were in grad school and she was still an adorably awkward college kid. But back then, I only saw her for occasional Seyfried family parties. And yeah, maybe I had a little crush, and enjoyed making her laugh way too much, but I thought I'd left all that behind.

Until now.

Having her in the office all week has seriously messed with my head.

Both of them.

If Ellie had any idea the kind of thoughts she stirs up—the kind of dreams that send me bolting for a cold shower at three in the morning, desperate for something to alleviate the ache and scrub my thoughts clean—my ass would've been hauled down to HR before the opening bell chimed on the stock exchange. And then she'd have her story gift wrapped with a bow, courtesy of my definitely-not-workplace-appropriate hard-on problem.

Fucking ironic, is what it is.

"...but that's all thanks to my high-level contacts in the energy and biotech industries."

I drag my attention back to Brian, who's supremely pleased with himself. Just like the last guy. And the woman before him.

The latest crop of MBA grads isn't lacking in confidence, that's for sure.

I let him natter on a bit longer, then wrap it up with a few noncommittal comments about next steps before I finally usher him out the door.

When my phone pings a minute later, I know I should probably be embarrassed at how fast I whip it out of my pocket, but I don't have time for that.

Shit. It's not Ellie.

It's her fucking big brother, like an omen from the universe warning me to cool it.

Just locked in the Cruise meeting. Dinner tomorrow night.

Great, I text back. *I'll let Rictor know.*

How are the interviews panning out? Anything promising? he asks.

No stand-outs. Setting up a few more next week.

Alright, keep me posted. Ellie giving you a hard time?

If he only knew. *Nothing I can't handle,* I text, then toss the phone onto my desk.

I'm trying to decide what the hell to do for lunch now that Ellie's off the menu, when in walks my assistant, Hannah. "Eric Webb here to see you?"

"Webb?" I flip through the candidate file on my desk. Nothing for Webb. "I thought we were done for today."

"Apparently this guy is a friend of Ian's. He says Ian called him from Portland, told him we'd squeeze him in?" She scrunches up her face, Hannah's classic *WTF* look. "I'm guessing this is the first you're hearing about it, too. And I'm also guessing you haven't eaten anything since that disgusting kale smoothie this morning."

"Yep. And nope." Figures. Ian's been so focused on the Portland office, it doesn't surprise me he forgot to mention the additional interview.

"Want me to blow him off and order your lunch?" she asks.

"No, that's not necessary. Send him in." Can't be worse than Brian "Six Sigma" Andover, and lunch can wait.

Gives me an excuse to wait a little longer for Ellie, too.

Pathetic, Holt. You need to get laid, and soon, before you make a fool of yourself.

The new guy steps through the door, attaché case in hand, his smile cool and guarded. He looks nervous—a touch gawky, too—wearing a suit that's a size too big and a mustache straight out of a 1970s porno.

"You'll have to forgive me." I move the folder in front of me to the side. "Ian didn't have a chance to send over your resume, Mr.—Webber, was it?"

"Webb." His voice cracks, but he clears his throat and tries again. "Eric Webb."

"Eric Webb." I stand up to shake the guy's hand, which is slim and surprisingly soft—definitely not into pumping iron, this one. "How do you know Ian?"

"At the risk of sounding cliche, he's a friend of the family," Webb says as we take our seats. "Our fathers went to Yale together. Frank was best man at my parents' wedding."

I nod, relaxing into my chair. Ian's dad Frank is a hard ass, but he's a good man, and definitely knows the business. If this guy is connected to Frank, he's gotta be good people.

"So. Why should I hire you, Eric?" I give him the fastball, no time for chit-chat. Guy doesn't miss a beat, though, fielding my questions with an ease his slightly unpolished appearance belies.

"You need me," he says matter-of-factly, "to diversify your strategic value proposition. You're getting great returns for your clients, generating lots of buzz on the street. But at the end of the day, you're still following the same old playbook."

I cross my arms and raise a brow. "Go on."

"I specialize in attracting and retaining risk-tolerant, high-net-worth clients looking for unconventional strategies in a time of market volatility and global instability. I've got a nose for emerging tech—we're talking *right* on the bleeding edge. Things most people have never even heard of outside of science fiction."

Webb has me on the hook now. Ian and I are always looking for ways to diversify our offerings, and offer our clients something unique. We deal mostly with athletes and celebs—people with lots of cash to play with, always hot for the next big thing.

If Webb can deliver on that, I want him on my team.

I ask him a few questions about his experience, letting him wax poetic about his ideal portfolio mix. He's got good instincts, the right blend of education and experience, and he absolutely knows his stuff.

But what I really need is a candidate who can think outside the MBA box and carry on a conversation about something other than ROI, APR, SEC, and the rest of the alphabet soup my analysts are swimming in.

I need someone who can charm clients and close deals.

I need someone creative, driven, and passionate.

I need someone who can take my mind off my best friend's little sister.

"What are you passionate about, Mr. Webb?" I interrupt a story about one of his former clients, surprising us both.

He waits a beat. Two. It's the first time he hasn't had a ready answer.

"P-Passionate?" he stammers.

"Yeah, something that lights you up inside, gets your juices flowing."

"Well, as I said, wealth management is—"

"Forget all that." I dismiss his comment with a wave. "I want to hear about the *real* you. Personally. Where do you spend your free time?"

"Personally?" He readjusts his tie, clearing his throat. "Well, I... I like the library."

Now we're getting somewhere. "A big reader, huh?"

At this, the guy lights up, a grin breaking his otherwise all-business demeanor. "If having my library card number memorized makes me a big reader, then yes." His mustache twitches with excitement, his eyes sparking with something almost *familiar*.

I can't put my finger on it, but there's something about this guy...

It's almost like we've met before. Maybe at one of Ian's family gatherings? He said their fathers were friends. Could that be it?

"Tell me the last thing you read for fun," I say, hoping to catch another glimpse of that spark.

"Dragon Spell." He says it like a challenge, as if he's daring me to laugh. When I don't, he continues, "It's about a wizard trying to resurrect a race of dragons, but he's the only person who believes they exist."

Webb goes on about the story, getting more amped up with every plot point. By the time he says, "...and then he discovers he's descended from dragon shifters," he's practically out of his chair with excitement.

In that moment, I know *exactly* why I recognize the spark in his eyes.

Because they aren't *his* eyes.

They aren't his *anything*.

Colored contacts, fake mustache, wig, the too-big suit and shoes...

Christ, I can't believe I didn't pick up on it sooner, but now that I have, it takes every ounce of willpower I possess to keep my expression neutral.

Because the candidate sitting across from me gushing about dragons?

Is none other than Ellie Seyfried in drag.

Do they still call it drag if it's a woman dressed as a man, rather than vice versa? I have no clue, but I know with absolute certainty that I've just been played.

Hard.

LIKE A BOSS is out now!
Learn more at Lili's website:
https://www.lilivalente.com/like-a-boss

ABOUT THE AUTHOR

USA Today Bestselling author Lili Valente has slept under the stars in Greece, eaten dinner at midnight with French men who couldn't be trusted to keep their mouths on their food, and walked alone through Munich's red light district after dark and lived to tell the tale.

Find Lili on the web at
www.lilivalente.com

SNOWBOUND WITH THE BILLIONAIRE

SNOWED IN WITH THE BOSS

MASQUERADE WITH THE MASTER

Bought by the Billionaire Series—

HOT novellas, must be read in order.

DARK DOMINATION

DEEP DOMINATION

DESPERATE DOMINATION

DIVINE DOMINATION

Kidnapped by the Billionaire Series—

HOT novellas, must be read in order.

FILTHY WICKED LOVE

CRAZY BEAUTIFUL LOVE

ONE MORE SHAMELESS NIGHT

Under His Command Series—

HOT novellas, must be read in order.

CONTROLLING HER PLEASURE

COMMANDING HER TRUST

CLAIMING HER HEART

Under His Command Trilogy-*USA Today* Bestseller

To the Bone Series—

Sexy Romantic Suspense, must be read in order.

A LOVE SO DANGEROUS

A LOVE SO DEADLY

A LOVE SO DEEP

Fight for You Series—

Emotional New Adult Romantic Suspense.

Read in order.

RUN WITH ME

FIGHT FOR YOU

Bedding The Bad Boy Series—must be read in order.

THE BAD BOY'S TEMPTATION

THE BAD BOY'S SEDUCTION

THE BAD BOY'S REDEMPTION

The Lonesome Point Series—

Sexy Cowboys written with Jessie Evans.

LEATHER AND LACE

SADDLES AND SIN

DIAMONDS AND DUST

12 DATES OF CHRISTMAS

GLITTER AND GRIT

SUNNY WITH A CHANCE OF TRUE LOVE

CHAPS AND CHANCE

ROPES AND REVENGE

8 SECOND ANGEL

Mazie tell him about the issues she and the other girls had been dealing with at their other job, and he was pretty cool with her. Hearing that he'd help her out of a bad situation made me think Mr. Brant was right to send me here. Maybe these tough, badass bikers might have a good side to them—at least one of them did. I tried to hold on to that thought as I walked into his office and told him I was looking for a job. Sadly, that comforting feeling went flying out the window the second I started taking off my clothes.

I didn't know the first thing about dancing or stripping. I'd never even undressed in front of a man—at least not in such an open manner, much less *stripped* for one in broad daylight. I was fairly certain Mr. Oh-so-sexy sitting behind the desk could see that I didn't have a clue what I was doing. I was absolutely mortified. It might not have been so bad if he hadn't been so damn good-looking with his stupid, smoking-hot build and piercing green eyes. He was one of those guys I could imagine seeing from across a crowded room and finding him staring back at me with one of those sultry expressions—like it was taking everything he had not to charge towards me and toss me over his shoulder, then carry me to his bed and have his way with me over and over again.

Sadly, he wasn't looking at me like that. In all honesty, I didn't know *how* he was looking at me.

Maybe it was pity or just plain curiosity, but it certainly wasn't with an animalistic desire flashing through his eyes. It made me want to crawl into a dark hole and escape this horrible nightmare that had become my life. As much as I wanted to get the hell out of there before I embarrassed myself even more, I couldn't. I needed money and I needed it fast.

This job was the best way for me to do that, so I pushed, "I'm really sorry. I could try again. I just...*if you...*"

"I've seen enough."

BE sure to check out Claiming Menace: Ruthless Sinners MC on Amazon...